ANDRE GONZALEZ

The Burden

Insanity #2

Paul,

Court is in session!

For Natasha

Let's keep this party going!

Contents

Also by Andre Gonzalez

Insanity (Insanity #1) – available on Amazon and BN.com
A Poisoned Mind – free at www.andregonzalez.net
Followed Home – available on Amazon and BN.com

I

Part One

1

Chapter 1

Monday, March 14, 2016

Jeremy Heston could feel it radiating from the other side of the polished oak door.

Destiny.

His throat swelled like a water balloon as nerves piled up in his empty stomach. After months of preparation, the time had arrived for Jeremy to face the world and put his experiment to the ultimate test. Three days after his rampage at the Open Hands office he looked down at his dark red prison uniform knowing a grueling road awaited. His hands were cuffed in front of his crotch and shackled to his matching ankle cuffs below, clanging around with each depressing step he took.

The door was a side entrance into the courtroom that would be his temporary home for the near future. Two officers stood on each side of him, ready to escort the mass murderer into the courtroom as soon as the judge ordered.

Over the weekend it occurred to him that he had never planned how to act in the courtroom, but used his newfound down time to devise a plan of attack. Sleep was impossible; he could feel the puffiness under his eyes and assumed heavy bags hung below his eyelids.

Stay quiet. Show no emotions. Don't look anyone in the eye. Poker face.

The entire experiment could fail if he made one misstep in the courtroom. If he wanted an acquittal based on the insanity plea, insanity was what he'd need to project every step of the way. *Give the people what they want.*

Being his first time out of his jail cell, his stomach growled in starvation. He hadn't eaten any of the food, only picking at some of the chips and crackers provided on the side. His mind had grown too consumed with what would come next that he forgot to eat.

The door in front of him swooshed open. "We're ready," a voice whispered from behind and the two officers put a hand on Jeremy's shoulders and guided him forward into the courtroom.

Cameras shuttered in rapid fire, snapping every breath Jeremy took as he walked toward his defense team. The table was only ten steps away but felt like a half marathon as he could hear the spectators murmuring beneath the sounds of the cameras. A woman broke out in sobs, heaving for air between her cries.

"Order in the court!" Judge Carlos Zamora banged his gavel, the room falling near silent. Judge Zamora sat at his elevated bench, his pudgy, light brown skin well hidden by his draped, black robe. The bright lights of the courtroom gleamed off his bald head as he stared at Jeremy from behind thick-framed glasses with empowering eyes that froze the mass murderer in place.

"Ladies and gentlemen, I understand the nature of this trial, but please remember this is still a court of law and rules will be enforced in this courtroom." The judge's voice boomed throughout the room, demanding an instant respect. He looked down and sifted through documents as the room hung in dead silence and anticipation.

Jeremy sat next to the lucky public defender assigned to him, Jenna Lane. She had stopped by late Saturday afternoon to introduce herself to Jeremy and informed him that his parents were looking into an attorney who specialized in mental health, but for the meantime she would get him through the preliminary hearing. Jeremy hadn't spoken one word to her, acting dazed and staring into space as she spoke.

Seeing Jenna for the second time, Jeremy wondered if the look of fear on her pale face was permanent or a mere reflex of his own presence next to her. She had looked terrified from the first time she visited him in jail and tried to speak with him. He remained silent and watched her scratch her black hair in frustration every time he ignored her.

"Mr. Heston," Judge Zamora said. "You are accused of committing thirteen murders, along with twenty-two counts of attempted murder. Due to the nature of the charges there will be no bail posted and you shall remain detained through the duration of your trial. Today is Monday the 14th of March, we will reconvene in one week for the formal charges against you. During that time you may have no visitors other than Ms. Lane, her staff, or any other counsel that she may consult with. Do you understand your rights?"

First test.

Jeremy stared in the judge's direction but avoided eye contact as he rocked back and forth in his seat.

"Mr. Heston, do you understand your rights?" Judge Zamora asked.

"We understand, your Honor," Jenna said, standing slender

5

and tall from her seat.

"Very well. Next week we'll also lay ground rules for media coverage in the courtroom moving forward. Court is adjourned." Judge Zamora banged his gavel, stood, and exited through his private door.

Chatter instantly erupted along with the resuming shutter of cameras. Jeremy looked down to his twiddling thumbs and felt Jenna staring at him.

Poor Jenna drew the short stick on this one, he thought. Jeremy presumed every single person tied to his case would always hold the case close in their memories. *History in the making,* he thought, and fought off a grin.

The bond hearing had lasted only seven minutes, but Jeremy felt like he had been in court for eight hours. The two officers returned to escort him back to his lovely jail cell where cold, gray walls and his single toilet waited for him. As he dragged his chains on the way out of the courtroom, he could feel hundreds of eyes burning into the back of his head, wanting so desperately for him to turn around. He kept his head down and wondered if his parents had been in the audience.

2

Chapter 2

Monday, March 14, 2016

Robert Heston sat at his kitchen table and reread the typed letter for the sixth time. He tugged on his necktie, still snug on his collar. He hated wearing a tie, but having sat in the front row in court, all eyes on him and his son, he'd had no choice. He only hoped his stubby beard and dark rings appeared natural on his exhausted face.

Where had they gone so horribly wrong as parents?

His wife, Arlene, had been in bed since Friday night when the news started spreading about Jeremy's killing spree, refusing to get out for anything aside from using the bathroom; she nibbled on snacks here and there but mostly hadn't been able to eat.

The phone hadn't stopped ringing the entire first day, so they left the landline off the hook and turned off their cell phones. The silence was better than the incessant ringing, but it allowed Robert's mind to wander. The TV was worse, his son's psychotic mugshot splattered across every news station.

The bundles of cash looked like something out of a movie. The bills were crisp, the white and mustard strap that held them together immaculate. Benjamin Franklin's expression looked extra stoic. Robert had never seen $200,000 in person before.

The typed note included in the large manila envelope was short and to the point:

Dear Heston family,

I'm sure this has all been very hard to digest, but don't give up. There is still hope to spare your son's life.

He'll never have a chance with a public defender, so I've included $200,000 as a gift for you to use toward a defense team. Your best bet is to contact Linda Kennedy from the Dobbs, Kennedy, and Irvine law firm. She's a well-established criminal defense attorney and has been known to perform miracles.

Sincerely,

A friend

Solid sleep had been hard to come by, but Robert was certain this was no dream. He thumbed through the bills, the slight breeze they made cooling his flushed face.

"Arlene, we really need to talk!" he shouted hopelessly down the hallway toward their bedroom. They had a discussion the night before regarding his wife's refusal to go to Jeremy's first court appearance; she lacked the energy and courage to face the world. Ever since they'd received word that her only child had slain over a dozen of his coworkers, shock and depression had taken hold of her emotions and left her useless.

At first, as the calls and texts started to come in, she was convinced she was the butt of a big prank. Her sweet Jer-Bear wouldn't harm a fly, and he had never mentioned buying a gun, so the messages all sounded like bullshit as far as she was concerned.

When she turned on the TV half an hour later and found every station covering the shooting at Jeremy's office, she still couldn't believe her son was the shooter, and her heart sank in fear that he might be injured. *They must have the story confused,* she thought of her friends' messages. Jeremy must have been hurt in the attack if everyone had reached out to her, so she started to call his cell phone, pacing around the living room. Three tries with no answer and sweat started to puddle under her arms.

Then the TV showed her son's face, an innocent, smiling face she had seen on his Facebook page at one point in time that always showed his close resemblance to Robert.

"The alleged shooter is Jeremy Heston," the reporter announced. "Jeremy, a former psychology student at Denver State University, is employed by Open Hands and is believed to have opened fire on his coworkers shortly before the lunch hour. He is currently in police custody and we will provide updates as soon as we receive them."

The announcer's voice faded into the background as Arlene felt the room spin around her. *This isn't happening. Impossible,* she thought.

As the facts were slowly released over the rest of the evening, Arlene felt her soul starting to numb. She had the urge to cry, but was frozen. All she wanted was to rewind the last day and go back to life the way it was the day before. Jeremy was over for dinner, they were all laughing and sharing stories, and life was normal.

But if everything the news said was true, normal was a long-gone concept, and would be for the rest of her life. How could she ever feel normal knowing her son had killed all those innocent people? She felt responsible, though she'd had no idea of Jeremy's violent urges.

Arlene had gone to bed to lie down, unable to keep up with her own racing mind, and ended up staying there for the next three days. She played through as many memories of Jeremy's childhood as she could remember, searching for anything that might suggest his recent actions. She felt weak, unable even to try to move around the house.

When she heard Robert shout for her from the down the hall, she heard a difference in his tone. It almost sounded like it had hope in it, though she wasn't sure what the hell he could be hopeful about. Robert had spoken to her multiple times since the news broke, but she'd found it difficult to focus on his words. Life had become a dream. She thought she could see herself from above at times.

Maybe it was time to get out of bed. Even getting dressed and brushing her teeth would be a big accomplishment. Her joints cracked and popped in protest as she swung her bony legs over the edge of the bed, feet dangling as they searched for the ground. When she stood, the room spun. She leaned against the wall to catch her balance.

The blinds and curtains were closed, leaving a soft glow as the only light. The stench of body odor filled the room, from her sweat-stained bedsheets. She had to brush back her brown hair that clung to the sides of her face.

Look at yourself, Arlene. This isn't you, she told herself. *Just like killing people isn't Jeremy,* she added. She slid her feet into a pair of slippers and dragged them out of the room and down the hall. The light in the living room sent a piercing pain through her retinas, making the back of her head throb in anger. She squinted while her eyes adjusted, and found Robert sitting at the kitchen table with a pile of money.

"Rob?" she asked, blinking rapidly to make sure she wasn't hallucinating. "What the hell is that?"

Her husband looked up at her. The last few days had taken a toll on his face, and heavy bags drooped below his eyes.

"Arlene, are you okay? I didn't think you'd actually get out of bed."

"I'm fine. What the hell is that?"

Robert looked from his wife to the pile of money. "It's $200,000."

"Where did it come from? What's going on?" Her voice had a slight accusatory tone.

"It was in this envelope in our mailbox," he said, patting the envelope next to the money. "With a note saying we should use the money to hire a defense attorney for Jeremy. The note is typed, no return address, no name."

"Is it real?"

"It's very real. I've counted it, and flipped to random bills and held them to the light. They all have the watermarks." Robert shook his head as he spoke, apparently still unable to believe it himself.

"Who would do this?" Arlene asked.

"I have no idea. I've been trying to think of anyone in our life that would even have this kind of money." Robert started to stack the bills in neat towers next to each other. "I can't think of anyone, can you?"

Arlene shook her head slowly. "So what are we gonna do with it?" she asked. "Should we tell someone?"

"Tell who? There's nothing to tell. We received a gift, that's all. I'm going to take this to the bank and deposit it before something happens to it, then I'm gonna call the lawyer in the note."

"Maybe she'll know something about it?"

"Doubt it. This is very much anonymous. Something's going on, but I'm not gonna sit back and watch Jeremy get sentenced to death."

Tears streamed from Arlene's eyes. She hadn't even let herself think ahead to the trial, where a group of strangers would decide their son's fate. Robert stood and embraced his wife, and felt her body soften as she gave in and started sobbing.

"It's going to be okay, honey," he said in a strong voice. "Apparently someone is on our side."

3

Chapter 3

Monday, March 14, 2016

Across town, Geoff Batchelor sat in his office at the Arapahoe County Office of the District Attorney. He had recently celebrated two years as the district attorney for the eighteenth Judicial District of Colorado, and sitting on his throne still felt as good as it had on the first day.

He was reading about the Open Hands shooting. After a morning of flipping through police reports, he wanted to read the raw stories told by the survivors.

His office faced downtown Denver to the north, the city's skyline a view he used to clear his mind and keep perspective when the world started to weigh down on him. He kept an organized office: nothing on his desk but his computer, a notepad, and a picture of his two little girls, both smiling wide, toothless grins. They had his blue eyes and blond hair, but otherwise they were spitting images of their mother—which made him cringe, thinking about the future boys that would be knocking down their door to date them.

"This is sick," Geoff said sharply. "We have to pursue the death penalty."

Karen Edson, the chief prosecutor for the case, sat across his desk nodding in agreement. She had stiff golden hair and a stone-faced expression, makeup caked over in an attempt to hide the years of stress from the job. She wore dark red lipstick that matched her boxy suit jacket.

"This may be as easy as it gets, to get the jury to vote death," she said.

"It's never easy," Geoff replied. "It only takes one juror to disagree. But the people want to see this guy dead, and it's our job to make that happen. Jury selection will decide everything."

Karen continued nodding. She and Geoff had a deep bond. After a couple years of working alongside her, she had become his most trusted confidante. He shared his fears, dreams, and personal matters with her. And although she kept to herself, she knew he was there for her as well. When Geoff secured the election and took control of the office, Karen was immediately promoted to his number two, where she kept him grounded and in check.

"Why not take the plea? Life in prison, some say, is even worse than lethal injection."

"It's the principle. Sure, he could rot in prison, but he killed thirteen people. I guarantee there are thirteen families that are tasting revenge for the first time in their lives. An eye for an eye."

"You sure this isn't about the governor race?" Karen asked with a smirk.

The seat for governor of Colorado was set to open up in 2018, and Geoff's name had already been thrown into the mix by numerous local analysts. He was fed up with the Democrats running things and wanted to take the state back to its conservative roots.

"This isn't about that."

We're going to be in the limelight. If we can get him executed, I'll be a hero, and that would make for an easy campaign.

Geoff had absolutely had the governor race in mind, as soon as he heard about the shooting on Friday afternoon. Fighting for justice would be easy in such a case. He had worked on plenty of cases where the defendant had murdered just one person, and the jury never sympathized. A case this extreme would only make it easier to convince the jury that the death penalty was the only way to go.

"I'll start prepping for a death penalty case and to counter an insanity plea," Karen said as she stood and rapped her long fingers on Geoff's desk before leaving his office. The district retained a death penalty specialist and they would need his services to prepare them for the trial.

Geoff returned his attention to his computer screen, shaking his head as he read the survivor accounts.

4

Chapter 4

Linda Kennedy hung up her phone and stared at her partner, Wilbert Dobbs, in disbelief.

"Who was that?" he asked in his croaky voice.

"That was Jeremy Heston's father."

"Heston? The office shooter?"

"Yeah. He asked me to defend his son. Said he doesn't wanna see him executed."

"Can they even afford you?"

"I told him my rate and estimated the whole trial could take a year, possibly more. He said he has the money."

Wilbert leaned back in the chair facing Linda's desk and scratched his chin. His life's work had taken its toll, creating bags under his eyes, wrinkles across his face, and turned his hair into a snowy white. He'd founded the defense firm almost forty years ago and had seen every type of case and client imaginable.

As he pushed into his late seventies, Wilbert had started to take a smaller role in the courtroom, and worked more as an adviser to his team of attorneys. They had the energy and drive;

he had the wisdom. That combination helped his firm win dozens of cases each year. A case like this, however, might be enough for him to polish his shoes and get back in the game.

"There's only one way out of this: insanity." He spoke confidently.

"Why should I even take this?" she asked. "There will be so many other cases to work on during the time this one case will take. I could be helping people who actually need it."

"Now, now, Linda. You have to look at the big picture here. Sure, he's guilty and everyone knows it. But think of the exposure. This case will be covered every night on the news. Your face will be all over. Avoiding the death penalty will be huge for your career. You'll have clients lining up around the block."

"We have no problem getting clients. We already have a rock-solid reputation."

"Then do it for the challenge. You're young still; you can handle this. It's a once in a lifetime opportunity. What if you actually got him off on insanity? It's a moonshot of a chance, but it's like the lottery: someone has to win it. I've won two cases in my life on insanity. It's truly an art to be able to convince twelve people to acquit someone based on an invisible science, when there's hard evidence right in front of them. I'll help you. I may even join your team if you'll have me."

He grinned as he looked her straight in the eye. She still looked great for forty-five, despite the silver streaks in her reddish hair. She stared back at Wilbert, her long face crunched in deep thought.

"Well, if you put it that way, what can I say?" Linda smiled. She had never worked on a trial with Wilbert, not directly at least. She had shadowed him in her early days with the firm, and assisted with trial preparation. But trying a case together had never been a possibility. But now, with her established as one of the best defense attorneys in town and him slowly on his way out, this might be her last chance to work with him.

"It won't be an easy case," Wilbert said, sitting up straight. "Batchelor is gunning for that governor seat and I guarantee he'll see this case as his golden ticket. Put the mass murderer on Death Row, win the hearts of the public, and even personally see to it that he isn't pardoned once elected."

"You're right. He'll never take a plea."

"No way. This could end up being a nationally televised trial. How often do these mass shooters hang around to face the music? Never. They always kill themselves—but not this guy. You have to be ready for the big stage that's going to come with this."

"Where do we even start?" Linda asked, genuinely unsure.

"We can go into more detail once everything is finalized, but an insanity case has very little to do with facts and more about telling a story to the jury. We'll drill deep down into this young man's life and find anything that could be stretched to make the jurors believe an insane person has always lived dormant within him."

"What about a psychologist?"

"Of course. Batchelor will have some hotshot from the state, and we can find one of our own to testify that our guy is nuts, but the jury usually sees through all that. No one witness or piece of evidence wins an insanity case—an attorney does. You have to pique the jury's interest from the opening statements and aggressively feed that interest. The more they feel he could be one of them, the more likely you are to get him off."

Linda nodded and rubbed her forehead.

"I know it sounds like a lot," Wilbert said. "But it's not as bad as you might think. The hard work starts now. Once you have your story painted, you just need to tell it."

"I've heard he hasn't spoken a word to his public defender. How am I supposed to defend someone who won't even talk?"

"He'll talk," Wilbert assured her. "He's leery about who to trust right now, but once he knows that his parents have hired you, he'll know he can confide in you."

Linda understood the crossroads awaiting her decision. A successful trial for Jeremy Heston would change her life.

"I'm going to defend Jeremy Heston," she said to herself, and Wilbert nodded in excitement.

* * *

"Hello?" an exhausted voice answered.

"Mr. Heston? This is Linda Kennedy. I wanted to follow up with you regarding your son's case."

"Hi, Ms. Kennedy. I appreciate the quick response."

"Not a problem. I understand this is a difficult time for you, and we need to get a plan in place. I've decided to defend your son and look forward to getting started right away."

"That's fantastic. We honestly didn't know who to turn to, but you kept coming up as the best in the state."

Linda ignored the compliment. "I was hoping to speak with you about the days leading up to this event. Do you have a few moments?"

"I still feel like I'm in a bad dream. Can we plan to meet later this week?" he asked.

"Yes, of course. We'll be back in court next Monday, where

the D.A. will formally press charges against your son. Can we plan to meet this Thursday or Friday?"

"Yes, Friday morning will work."

"Perfect. I'll send you the directions to our office and some of the questions I'll be asking, so you can refresh your memory."

"Thank you, Ms. Kennedy. Is there any chance my son won't be executed?"

"Please, call me Linda. And yes, there is a good chance we can spare his life. We'll be working tirelessly to ensure the death penalty doesn't happen."

"Thank you. I'll see you on Friday."

Linda dropped her handset into its cradle. *Jeremy's parents must be sick at what their son has done.* Linda had no kids, but she was sure no one raised their child to be a mass murderer.

She pulled up Jeremy's mugshot on her computer. His hair was in brown waves surrounding his pale face. His eyes were wide, almost dilated, and he smirked, his lips tight. He looked every bit the lunatic she wanted him to be.

"What happened to you? Where did it all go wrong?"

She would need to look deep into his past, to see what had led to Jeremy opening fire on his entire office. People didn't just wake up one day and decide to commit mass murder.

5

Chapter 5

Thursday, March 17, 2016

Jeremy lay on his cot, staring at the gray ceiling as he had for countless hours over the weekend. The few minutes in court had been more intense than he'd anticipated. A lot of people were crowded into that courtroom and would be throughout the entire trial.

I should have studied more about the justice system. A knowledge of the courts wouldn't necessarily have helped him directly, as the trial was in the hands of the attorneys, but he would've felt better prepared to handle the situation. Even though his only job would be to sit there and appear crazy, it would be nice to know what would come next. Perhaps his defender could fill him in.

If I told her what I was doing, would she believe me? Would it affect the way she fought this case?

Jeremy closed his eyes and played back the events from last Friday, where they would be etched forever in his memory. The jail cell gave way to the office, where he could feel the death spewing from his hands, through the rifle. The screams and cries for help would always echo in his mind.

He saw his coworkers lying on the ground, pools of blood forming beneath their limp bodies. Some bled from their mouth and stared lifelessly at the ceiling, others twitched and trembled as they clung to life. He'd never forget the symphony of ringtones when the news had broken across the country as he sat handcuffed in a whirlwind of police and dead bodies. They had kept him handcuffed to a desk while the dozens of officers scrambled to save lives and preserve evidence.

A tear rolled down his cheek as he imagined Sylvia dead on the floor. Her nine-year-old son must be terrified. If Jeremy ever got to see the light of day again, he would find her son, to explain and apologize.

"Heston!" a voice barked, snapping Jeremy out of his daydream. An officer stood at the barred door, holding a tray through the slot. "Come get it."

It seemed a different officer had brought him his meals each time.

Jeremy stood from his bed and approached the bars, grabbing the tray. It was filled with some sort of mashed potatoes and a ham sandwich that looked to have come from roadkill.

It's time to snap out of your daze and start selling this insanity.

Jeremy offered a wide grin to the officer before returning with his tray of food to his cot.

"You think this is a game?" the officer said under his breath.

Jeremy sat and put the sandwich in his mouth, not breaking eye contact with the officer before he walked away, cursing to himself.

That was easy.

* * *

An hour later, Jeremy entered the visitation room, escorted by yet another officer, who remained a few feet behind him as he sat down on the metal stool. The room housed five booths, each with a glass divider and a phone in a cradle. There were no other visitors at the moment, except for the middle-aged woman sitting behind the glass.

At the sight of him, Linda stood, revealing a form-fitting gray pantsuit. Jeremy had a dazed look of confusion, likely expecting to see Jenna, his public defender, instead. The sight of the mass murderer sent a shockwave of nerves through Linda's body. *Keep your eyes on the prize, he's a client like anyone else,* she reminded herself.

Jeremy looked back to the officer, who gestured for him to sit.

He took his seat and lifted the phone from its cradle, pulling it slowly toward his ear with an absent stare through the glass. "Hello?" he said quizzically.

"Hi, Jeremy, my name is Linda Kennedy. I've been hired by your parents to defend you. I'm hoping you can talk with me today. I need to hear your side of the story if you want any chance of surviving this trial." She spoke confidently.

She sat back and watched him. He leaned closer to the glass before speaking.

"Hi, Linda. What happened to Jenna?" His voice came through mysterious and creepy.

"Jenna was assigned to you as a public defender. She's been relieved of her duties as I'll be taking over," she said, fully in control.

"Lucky lady." Jeremy's comment sent chills down Linda's

23

spine, reminding her of Hannibal Lecter's first encounter with Clarice. Was Jenna the lucky one? Or herself? He still had that blankness in his eyes that she'd seen—that everyone had seen—in his mugshot.

"And what kind of results have you had?" Jeremy questioned.

"Murder is always difficult when there's DNA evidence, but I've had two successful cases where my client walked free."

Jeremy nodded. "Well, I did the crime, no point in arguing that I didn't. As you may know, I was in school for psychology, close to graduating with my master's. I've had plenty of time to think over the last few days, and I believe I suffered from some sort of psychotic episode. Schizophrenia runs in my family."

Linda was caught off guard by him being so forthcoming. She scribbled notes to later share with the psychologist.

"Thank you for sharing that. So that you know what to expect: the D.A. will pursue the death penalty and we're going to counter with a plea bargain of life in prison. Is that something you're okay with?"

Jeremy leaned back and scrunched his face in thought. "So we're not gonna fight it?"

"We will. It's all posturing at the beginning. We know the D.A. wants the death penalty, so he won't take a plea bargain. I'd call it a one percent chance that he takes our plea. When he doesn't, we'll then move forward with an insanity defense."

"You think I'm insane?" Jeremy fought back the excitement in his voice.

"It's the only fight we have in a case like this. We'll have some psychologists run tests."

Jeremy nodded.

"I hope you understand there's a real possibility that the jury will ask for the death penalty. People are not going to feel sympathy for you."

Jeremy said, "I understand. I hope they'll come to understand the nature of mental illness. When will the trial start?"

"It's hard to say. Jury selection may take some time. Since this is a case with mental illness at the forefront, there will be a lot of interviews between you and different doctors. There's also thousands of pieces of evidence to process and file. I think the soonest we can start trial is six months from now, and that's a stretch."

Jeremy nodded. He'd known there would be a long waiting period between his arrest and the trial. There always seemed to be a lag time in murder cases.

"How long do you think the trial will run?"

Linda paused to remind herself that she was speaking with the man who had just murdered thirteen people at his office.

"I would guess two months at the most, possibly one full month. There will be tons of witnesses giving testimony, and like I said, around one thousand pieces of evidence that will each need to be discussed."

Linda started in with her own questions. "I'm meeting with your parents tomorrow. Is there anything you want me to pass along to them?"

"When will I get to see them in person?"

"Right now that's up to the judge's discretion. For the time being I'm your only permitted visitor. I'd imagine he'll grant your parents visitation rights, but it's impossible for me to know when."

"Okay. Tell them hello for me and that I'm okay." Jeremy's request was in sharp contrast to his chilling tone.

Come back to reality, she told herself. *He can't hurt you.*

"Jeremy, I need to know why you did it. How long have you

been planning this?"

Without hesitation, he replied, "I had an episode. I don't recall much of it. I remember going to work that morning, but then things get fuzzy. Then I was being handcuffed and there were bodies all over the floor."

She stared at him, her eyes full of doubt. "Look, if I'm going to defend you I need to know everything. I need to know how things happened from your perspective. I need to know what was going on in your mind. I need to know how the air smelled when you woke up that morning. We can't afford any surprises in this trial."

"I'm afraid I've told you what I remember. I'll think some more on it, but that's all I got.

Linda sighed. "Okay. I'll be in touch." She hung up the phone, wrote another note, and stormed out of the visitation room.

Still at square one, she thought. She would need to consult with a doctor on the validity of Jeremy's claims. Her gut told her Jeremy Heston was full of shit.

6

Chapter 6

Friday, March 18, 2016

"Thank you for meeting with me today, Mr. and Mrs. Heston," Linda said as they all sat in her office. Both Robert and Arlene had dark circles under their eyes. Linda doubted they were even aware of their appearance, and she didn't blame them one bit. "I met with Jeremy yesterday afternoon, and I think it went well, all things considered."

Robert sat up straighter, curious.

"He mentioned schizophrenia runs in your family. Is that correct?"

Robert rubbed his white goatee, eyebrows raised in surprise. "My grandfather was schizophrenic. It's in our family's medical history." He shrank back into his seat, looking disappointed.

"I see. We'll talk more about that in a bit. I'm curious about the last time you saw Jeremy, before all this happened?"

Arlene's eyes welled with tears at the question, her lips starting to quiver. "He was at our house the night before the shooting, for dinner. Last Thursday." She couldn't contain her tears anymore. Linda pushed her a box of tissues.

"How was he acting?" Linda directed the question to Robert.

"Normal. For the most part. We talked sports, talked about work. He didn't finish his dinner, just picked at it. It seemed like something was bothering him, but he told us that he was feeling sick. We didn't think anything of it."

Linda heard a waver in Robert's voice and decided to redirect her questioning. "Tell me more about your grandfather, Mr. Heston." She kept her tone soft and compassionate.

"Yes," Robert said. "My grandfather suffered from paranoid schizophrenia. We've rarely discussed him—I'm surprised Jeremy remembered that, to tell you the truth. But to make a long story short, my grandfather thought he lived in a different reality and acted out in strange ways."

"Ever violent?"

"Not that I know of. He may have said violent things, but never actually harmed anyone, that I know of."

"Do you have medical records showing he was diagnosed with schizophrenia?"

"No medical records, but I think my grandmother had him admitted into a mental institution. They would likely have records on file."

"I would appreciate you tracking those down for me. It may go a long way toward making sure your son is not executed."

Arlene, who had calmed down a little, burst out sobbing.

"We can do that," Robert said, patting his wife's back. "What do you honestly see happening in this trial?"

Linda gathered her thoughts, choosing her words carefully.

"This is a difficult case. I won't beat around the bush. There's a strong chance your son will be sentenced to death. My team is going to focus on not letting that happen. If we can get sympathy from just one juror, his life will be spared. It requires a unanimous vote for someone to be sentenced to death. It's easier said than done, but it's possible. The last death penalty sentence was for the man who shot his coworkers at the Chuck E. Cheese in the '90s."

Robert nodded and Arlene sniffled.

"I'm going to prepare some questions for you both to answer later. Likely next week," Linda said. "The questions will be focused on Jeremy's childhood and upbringing. Answer as truthfully, and with as much detail, as you can. Take your time—we prefer complete, accurate responses over quick responses. This will be our first step in diagnosing your son, and will tell us where to go next with the doctors."

"Yes, of course," Robert said. "Please let us know what else we can help with."

"Thank you, I'll definitely be in touch. Don't forget Jeremy's next court date is Monday."

Linda shook their hands and walked them out of her office.

* * *

Monday, March 21, 2016

Jeremy sat in the courtroom next to Linda. It wasn't as packed as the initial hearing had been, but there were still a lot of people. The cameras shuttered like before, but calmed down as the judge entered and took his seat.

"Mr. Heston, will you please stand?" Judge Zamora asked. Jeremy stood, feeling the eyes of the world on him. "Today will be fairly quick. I will read the charges being brought against you by the state, and we will schedule future hearings regarding your case."

Judge Zamora opened an envelope handed to him by the court clerk. He peered over the papers, flipping through them as if reading a book.

"Mr. Heston, the state of Colorado charges you with twenty-six counts of first degree murder, forty-four counts of attempted murder, and one count of inciting violence. To be clear, the counts of first degree murder are broken into two: thirteen counts of murder with deliberation and thirteen counts of murder with extreme indifference. Mr. Heston, you have the right to a preliminary hearing within thirty-five days—do you wish to exercise this right?"

Jeremy turned to Linda, clueless as to what this meant. She stood beside him.

"We waive the right for a preliminary hearing, Your Honor."

She sat back down in a swift movement.

"Very well. Due to the nature of this case, I presume your defense will require some time to prepare, Ms. Kennedy, so we'll plan to reconvene here on the fifth of July for a pre-trial hearing. Please be prepared to have a plea bargain by then, should you choose. Are there any questions from counsel?"

Linda shook her head, as did Geoff Batchelor across the aisle.

"Court is adjourned." The judge banged his gavel and rose from his throne.

Chatter flooded the courtroom, cameras returned to snapping, and Linda leaned over to Jeremy and said, "This is all normal, nothing to worry about."

He mentally tallied the charges: seventy-one in total. *Not too shabby.* Three figures would have been better, but no point in being greedy at this point in the game.

He could hear people conversing behind his back, wondering about his mental state, his motivation—and others wishing him dead. But that just reassured him: this case could change the world.

This must be what it feels like to be a star.

Chapter 7

Monday, March 28, 2016

The day had come for Jeremy's biggest test, and the biggest threat to his experiment. He would meet with Dr. William Reed, a forensic psychiatrist from Delaware, hired by the prosecution to interview Jeremy, over the course of one week, to gauge his mental state.

Dr. Reed had worked as a forensic psychiatrist for two decades, doing work with the FBI and CIA, and on criminal cases around the world. Jeremy wouldn't be able to bullshit his way through a week with Dr. Reed.

Lay the groundwork. Stay insane.

Linda had informed him that there would be two sets of interviews, with two different psychiatrists, one for the prosecution and one for the defense.

"Just stay truthful," she told him. "Dr. Reed is being hired to prove that you're legally sane. Answer honestly. These interviews will be recorded and shown in court. Your answers need to be consistent with those you give to the doctor we hire later on."

Jeremy waited in an interrogation room, a lone light hanging above. The walls were white and a square table stood in the center, with a chair on each side. Jeremy sat in the chair that faced the door and a camera mounted on a tripod. The small space reminded him exactly of the interrogation rooms he'd seen on TV where two officers typically play the game of good cop, bad cop.

New walls to look at is always a big day. Just stay relaxed and stick your story. NO PREMEDITATION!

The door swung open and an old man entered. He wore a black suit with a yellow shirt and black tie. His white hair clung to the sides of his head, a few stragglers on top.

"Hello there, Mr. Heston," he said in a friendly voice, pushing his glasses to the top of his nose. "My name is Dr. William Reed. I don't mind at all if you call me Bill."

He sat down in the chair across from Jeremy and opened a briefcase to grab a thick folder of papers.

"Alright. We'll be meeting every day this week for five hours. I'll be evaluating your mental state. The end goal is to determine your state of mind at the time of the shootings and the events leading up to that day. So I'll ask you a question, and all you need to do is respond with your honest answer. Is that clear?"

Jeremy nodded. *Here we go. Remember, you snapped, nothing was planned. Nothing was planned. Nothing was planned.* He drilled the thought into his mind, knowing one slip up could ruin his life.

The interview dragged for hours as planned. Jeremy wanted to pluck his eyeballs after a couple of hours hearing the monotone of Dr. Reed.

"Mr. Heston, did you have many friends as a child?" the

doctor asked bluntly.

"Yes. I've always had a good circle of friends."

"Did you have close friends at the start of 2016?" The doctor looked at Jeremy, emotionless, while a hand continued to write notes.

"Yes. Some of the best friends I've ever had."

"When you were a child, say around age seven, did you ever have a fascination with bugs?"

"Bugs?"

"Yes, did you like to play with bugs outside?"

What the fuck do bugs have to do with anything?

"Sure, I played with bugs."

He quickly realized the game plan for the week. Ninety percent of Dr. Reed's questions today focused on Jeremy's childhood, and he didn't once bring up the shooting. He figured the week would progress through Jeremy's life, with Friday being the day he'd be grilled on the actions of March 11.

What was this called? The M'Naghten test? He remembered learning about it in school, during a Forensic Psychology course.

"Did you ever kill the bugs?"

There it is.

"No."

Jeremy responded with quick and short answers, not elaborating on anything unless the doctor asked him to. The less detailed he was, the less likely a statement could come back later to bite him in the ass.

The doctor's voice droned on throughout the afternoon as he weaved questions about 2016 into the plethora of childhood questions. They even shared lunch together while the process continued. Jeremy wondered what would happen if he reached over the table and tried to head-butt the uptight doctor. He would have loved to strangle him with his shackles, but those were chained to the ground. Best-case scenario if he harmed the doctor, Jeremy would spend life in prison doing work for an angry warden, counting the days till he died. The world would move on and his name would be a footnote in a long history of mental health and gun violence.

"Thank you, Jeremy. I think today was very productive," Dr. Reed said at the end of their first session. He stacked his papers inside the briefcase and clasped it shut. "I'll see you tomorrow to continue. Have a good rest of your day."

Jeremy waited in the interrogation room for a few minutes before an officer arrived to take him back to his cell.

His brain burned from the five hours of questions. Just a couple weeks of not using his mind and he'd already lost some of his sharpness. He'd need to mentally prepare for the rest of the week. And then Linda had mentioned more interviews would be lined up within the month. Now that he had an idea of how these interrogations flowed, he could better prepare for the upcoming days and the next doctor. He longed for a notebook to help keep his thoughts organized, but would have to make do with his trusty mind.

He thought the first session with Dr. Reed had gone well, but he couldn't know for sure. Jeremy's basic knowledge of psychology paled in comparison to Dr. Reed—who would have obtained a medical doctorate after years of studying and a residency.

Jeremy lay down for the rest of the day and slept through the dinner placed in his cell.

8

Chapter 8

Monday, April 11, 2016

Robert's hands trembled as he held a new manila envelope. He could tell what was in it by its massive bulge. It was an unmarked envelope addressed to him, just as the last had been, and there was more money inside.

He looked around the neighborhood and found no one in sight. He'd gotten used to being home all day and enjoying the silence while the rest of the world went to work. He had enough saved for retirement, and if money kept arriving in envelopes he just might propose to Arlene that they run off and leave all their problems behind.

She'll never leave Jeremy. Not without a resolution one way or the other.

Robert had started to hate his son. He watched the news every night and surfed the internet throughout the day, to find any new information on Jeremy's crime and trial. Even though he was the father of the defendant, he was pretty much left out of the loop, unless he placed a call to the defense attorney. Even she was pretty tight-lipped.

The internet had plenty of resources, along with lots of opinion pieces and fake news. Robert had found a fan group that had formed on multiple social media platforms. They called themselves "Heston's Homies" and they glorified the murders, claiming Jeremy had done the right thing, fighting back against society. These boys and girls, mostly teenagers, all but worshiped his imprisoned son.

Some of the girls posted about writing to Jeremy, saying how much they'd love to date him, even if he was in jail. One crazed fangirl even said she wanted to have Jeremy's baby. The whole thing made Robert choke down vomit, as he explored the group's multiple pages and hundreds of followers.

Once there was a verdict, whether Jeremy received a life sentence or the death penalty, they would *have* to leave Colorado if they were to find any sort of peace. Staying in town would be impossible; people already shot Robert dirty looks when he was out running errands. Life would never be normal for them again, in the city where they both had been born and raised.

He went inside and sat down on the living room couch, dropping the envelope with a thud on the coffee table. "Arlene!" he shouted. "We got another envelope."

Arlene still spent most of her time in the bedroom watching TV, though she'd begun to eat lunch and dinner with Robert at the kitchen table. They'd even watched a movie together the week prior, though they both had trouble focusing on it.

Arlene walked into the living room and gasped at the sight of the envelope. "How much is in it? Is there another note?" she asked, walking faster to join Robert on the couch.

"I haven't looked yet." He ripped the top of the envelope open. Poking out was a letter, which he pulled out and unfolded, flattening it on his lap. It was, once again, typed.

Dear Heston family,

Please use the enclosed gift to help with your son's trial. Let your defense team know you would like to hire the best available psychiatrist, Dr. Ana Brown. No one is a bigger proponent for mental health than her.

I think your son has a real shot in this trial. Don't give up hope.

A friend

Robert put the note back on the coffee table and pulled out the bundles of money. He counted fifty bundles in total: $500,000.

"What the hell?" he said, looking at Arlene. "Who's doing this?"

Arlene made the sign of the cross. "I think someone is looking over our family. There's no other explanation."

Robert wasn't sure what to believe, but after receiving a total of $700,000 in the mail he felt anything was possible.

"Do you think anyone will ask us about this?" Arlene asked. "The IRS?"

"I have no idea. All we can do is tell them the truth if they do ask."

Arlene sobbed and sat back on the couch with her hands over her eyes. "What does it all mean? Are we supposed to just keep giving this mystery money to Jeremy's legal team?"

Robert decided he had to at least try for what he really wanted. "We could sit on the money, stash it away for later, and start a new life with it after the trial. Or we can give it to Linda, to spend on this new doctor."

"The person who gave it to us thinks he has a real shot. I

think we need to trust them and spend the money how they say."

Robert had known she would say this. He gulped his response back, knowing the money would be better utilized for their future.

"Alright then. That's what we'll do," he said. "I'll call Linda."

* * *

"This keeps getting weirder," Linda said as she sat down across from Wilbert in his office. "The Hestons want us to reach out to Ana Brown in Arizona, to interview Jeremy and be our witness."

"Ana Brown?" Wilbert sat up in his chair and closed his laptop. "She's got to be more expensive then you. They have the money for this?"

"Robert Heston told me to do 'whatever it takes' to get his son freed."

"Freed?" Wilbert gasped. "How rich are these people? Don't they live in Larkwood? They can't have that much money."

"I looked them up. They make a little over six figures combined. They either have an inheritance, or they're spending their life savings on this trial."

"Well, it doesn't really matter—if they have money, then we have a real chance. If we get Ana Brown on board, anything can happen. We need to start thinking bigger than just fighting for a life sentence. This is your opportunity—you need to get on the next flight to Phoenix and meet with Dr. Brown. Don't leave until she agrees to work on this case."

9

Chapter 9

Tuesday, April 12, 2016

Dr. Ana Brown sat in her office, waiting for the lawyer to arrive. The phone call she'd had yesterday with Linda Kennedy had intrigued her. Jeremy Heston would be a fascinating mind to study, but would also require a lot of time, possibly the next three months. She would need to find someone to take on her several dozen patient appointments. A temporary move to Denver would also be required.

But if the lawyer insisted on flying to Phoenix to meet her in person, then they meant business. And if they meant business, that meant serious money. With her fourth psychology book set for release and a monthly speaking appearance scheduled for every month of the year, money wasn't really a concern. However, Jeremy Heston could provide enough material for a whole book on his own.

She also had a tropical trip planned for her sixty-fifth birthday, in October. No way would she reschedule that. Every year she planned a trip for her birthday.

What would be driving this lawyer? Did she share the passion for getting both convicted and accused criminals the help they deserved? Or was she just looking out for herself, trying to win an impossible case?

A soft knock came from her office door.

"Come in!" she shouted from across the room. She pushed aside the stacks of folders that had accumulated over the week to clear space on her desk.

The door opened and a slender woman entered, wearing a tailored pantsuit and flashy jewelry. It reminded Dr. Brown of how she herself had dressed when she was in her early fifties, which she judged the lawyer to be.

"Ms. Kennedy?" Dr. Brown asked as she stood.

"Yes. It's a pleasure to meet you, Dr. Brown," Linda said as she hurried toward the desk. The women shook hands and sat down opposite each other, across the desk. "I appreciate you taking the time to meet with me."

"Of course. I'm always happy to discuss how my expertise might help someone in need."

"I'm glad to hear that, because we really need your help. You may know of my client, Jeremy Heston."

"I do. Quite the tragedy. How were you thinking I might be able to help?" Dr. Brown knew very well what the lawyer was going to ask, but wanted to stay in control of the conversation.

"We would like you to assess Mr. Heston's mental state as we prepare for trial, and also serve as a witness, to testify on your findings."

"Are you assuming I'll just say he's insane and build a story around that?"

"Of course not. Though we have had other doctors run tests and they agree there is something wrong with him mentally. We believe you'll be able to confirm those findings. That,

41

combined with your credentials, could help us make a strong case to keep a mentally ill man out of prison. And of course, off death row."

"What does your timeline look like?" Dr. Brown kept her tone casual.

"We would like to have the assessment done as soon as possible. It's April now, and we're most likely looking at a trial at the end of the year."

"When, exactly?" Dr. Brown demanded.

Linda pulled out her cell phone and Dr. Brown could see her hand trembling as she flipped through her virtual calendar. "I should know for sure in July, but I'm anticipating opening statements sometime in November or December."

Dr. Brown flipped open the laptop on her desk and opened her own calendar. "That should work."

"If you need more time, we can always request a delay. We don't want you to feel rushed by any means."

"What is your client willing to pay?"

"The Heston family seems to have some money saved. We were going to propose $250,000 for your services, plus travel expenses and accommodations."

"Are you expecting to keep me retained during the entire trial?"

"Yes. My team would like to consult with you throughout the trial and prep. We won't need you in Denver, however, aside from your actual testimony and testing. We're fine consulting with you over the phone."

"Make it $350,000 and you have a deal."

"Done."

"Perfect. Give me next week to make arrangements here in Phoenix and I'll plan to be in Denver on the eighteenth."

"Terrific. That will be plenty of time for me to arrange for your interviews at the jail. Is there anything you need us to provide?"

"No, not right now, but thank you. I'll make sure to send everything I need ahead of time. If you can just keep it all stored for me."

"I'll personally keep it in my office until you arrive." Linda handed her business card over.

"Thank you. Was there anything else you needed from me today?"

"No, Doctor, thank you again for your time."

10

Chapter 10

Wednesday, May 18, 2016

Geoff and Linda stood in Judge Zamora's chambers. A soft golden glow splashed across the room through the sheer white curtains hanging over the window. A sturdy oak desk sat in front of the windows, where the judge sat in a leather chair that looked more like a throne. Geoff studied the hundreds of books lined up on the wall.

"Thank you both for stopping in today," Judge Zamora said, removing his glasses and dropping them on his desk. "I want to discuss a couple matters."

The attorneys remained standing and watched the judge as he stared at them.

"The first matter is regarding the press coverage for this trial. I've decided to allow one camera to record the entire trial. The jury will be left out of the camera's view, but the rest of the courtroom is fair game."

Linda smirked. "Great exposure for the governor here."

"Don't call me that," Geoff said through clenched teeth.

"Stop it!" the judge barked. "I don't need your bullshit in my chambers, we're here to talk business. You've both been behaving so far, I expect nothing different when testimony begins. This is a sensitive case that will have national attention and I expect both of you to be positive representatives of our legal system. I won't hesitate to hold either of you in contempt if there are any outbursts. Are we clear?"

"Yes, Your Honor," Geoff murmured like a punished child.

Linda nodded. She loved getting a reaction from the district attorney.

"Are there any objections to the camera?"

They shook their heads.

"Perfect. Now, the other issue is one I've been losing sleep over: jury sequestration. You have both submitted requests for a sequestration, but I've ultimately decided against it."

"Your Honor, I think that's a mistake. Especially if there's going to be a camera in the courtroom," Geoff pleaded, taking a step toward the oak desk. Linda decided to let Geoff take the bullet for them. They had submitted the request in anticipation of the constant press coverage the trial would receive. Having the jury locked away from the outside world would help both sides, by preventing any external information from making its way into the jury's minds.

"I understand your reasons for wanting it, but it's already going to be extremely hard to find a jury. Sequestration makes it even harder, as you know, by limiting the pool of jurors. Aside from that, sequestered juries are known to make quick decisions on the verdict. After a long trial, being locked up in a hotel with limited contact to the outside world, all they want to do is go home. I feel allowing them to go home each day will help us arrive at a fair verdict."

"It's too risky," Geoff continued. "Someone will see something they're not supposed to."

"Then I suggest you pick trustworthy jurors, Mr. Batchelor," the judge snapped. "We'll have protocol in place during the jury's time in the courtroom. Absolutely no cell phones allowed in the building."

Geoff wanted to plead further, Linda could see, but decided against it.

"Now, will either of you be filing any objections to this?" the judge asked, practically daring them.

"No, Your Honor," Linda said.

Geoff turned red and shook his head in disgrace.

"Very well," Judge Zamora said. "Mr. Batchelor, you may leave. I have a couple of motions to discuss with Ms. Kennedy."

"Thank you, Your Honor," Geoff said and turned for the door.

"Bye, Governor," Linda said.

Geoff hesitated, shook his head, and stepped out of the room.

The judge had a smirk on his face when Linda turned back to him.

"Ms. Kennedy, I received your motion about the defendant's dress code. I'll allow him to dress in street clothes and be free of handcuffs and shackles. We'll have him wear a harness underneath his clothing that will be anchored to the ground."

"Thank you, Your Honor."

"This is a big opportunity for you, Ms. Kennedy. Win or lose, this can change your life. Remember: the whole country will be watching." The judge winked at her then turned his attention to the large calendar splayed across his desk.

"Thank you, Your Honor. I look forward to it."

Chapter 11

Tuesday, July 5, 2016

"We have a few matters to cover today," Judge Zamora said, "so I expect us all to get to the point."

It was the morning of Jeremy's preliminary hearing, and he sat at Linda's side. His parents sat in the front row of the gallery; he had locked eyes with his mom before quickly looking to the ground. He had to remain emotionless. The sight of his mother forced him to fight away the growing lump in his throat that always accompanied crying. She looked exhausted and miserable, despite a sharp outfit and perfect makeup. He could see the pain in her eyes.

His father refused to meet his eye, looking down at his lap. Through all his planning, Jeremy had never really considered the effects his actions would have on his parents. Seeing them in such visible pain forced a flood of tears that he held back behind his eyeballs.

The judge continued, "The first matter I would like to address is regarding the press coverage for this trial. I've decided to allow one camera in the courtroom for the duration of the trial. The workings of our justice system should always be available for public viewing. Since this case already has a national following, I'm allowing the trial to be shared. The camera will be set up in the back, facing me, and not showing the jury box. We will restrict the amount of press allowed in the courtroom." The judge spoke to the press that filled the back of the courtroom. Most of them nodded, expecting such a decision.

"My clerk will be in touch with the members of the press, to grant some of you passes, and the remainder of you will have to follow along on TV. We will open a separate viewing room should you wish to still be in the courthouse, but I want to save space for the victims and families of the deceased to attend this trial."

The judge turned to Linda. "Now, Ms. Kennedy, you had something to bring to the court's attention?"

Linda stood, wearing a purple pantsuit that revealed curves Jeremy hadn't noticed before.

"Yes, Your Honor. The defense would like to request more time in preparing our case. We believe our client to be mentally ill and need more time to assess the nature of his illness."

"And what have you been doing since we last met in March?" the judge demanded.

"Your Honor, our client has now met with two different psychiatrists: one appointed by the state and one by the defense. Each doctor met with our client for twenty hours of interviews. As you can imagine, we have a lot of reading and research to conduct, based on these interviews alone. We're working as fast as we can, but between the interviews and the mountain of evidence being presented, it's been impossible to complete our due diligence for the defendant."

"Any objections, Mr. Batchelor?" the judge asked the district attorney.

"No, Your Honor. We're still evaluating the reports ourselves," Geoff said.

"Very well then," Judge Zamora said. "We will plan on a follow-up hearing on Monday, September 19. Please be prepared then to discuss evidence being submitted for this case."

"Thank you, Your Honor," Linda said, and sat back down.

"Is there anything else that needs to be discussed today?" Judge Zamora asked. Geoff and Linda shook their heads. "Court is adjourned."

* * *

Linda followed Jeremy to the jailhouse.

"We're going to stall as long as we can," she told him through the phone. "It's part of our strategy."

"How so?" Jeremy asked.

"These events are still too fresh in the public's eye. And since the judge denied our request to transfer this case outside of the county, your jurors are going to be selected from this community. I want to put as much time between March 11th and the start of the trial as possible, to take the sting out of the situation."

"Exactly how long are you thinking?"

"I think I can buy us another year, possibly two."

"Two years!" Jeremy gasped. "Is that really necessary?"

"Jeremy. You slaughtered thirteen people and wounded

dozens more. I would love to stall five years, but that's simply not possible."

Jeremy clenched his teeth and felt blood rush to his face, a sensation he had felt toward Shelly before he pulled the trigger on her. Sometimes he felt Linda was his greatest shot. Other times, he thought she was full of shit and should quit her profession. This was one of the latter instances.

"What have you found from the interviews with the shrinks?"

"We're still sorting through all of that, as I mentioned in court, but it looks like Dr. Brown diagnosed you with a severe case of psychosis. The prosecution's doctor stated that you are legally sane, as expected."

Psychosis. That's an easy cop-out—a blanket statement that covers all kinds of disorders.

Jeremy nodded. "Is there any sort of treatment I can receive?"

"Yes. We have two options for that. You can either go through another interview process with the state's psychiatrist and they can set up a treatment plan and prescribe drugs. Or we could have a hearing with the doctors who already interviewed you, and get them to all agree on what your treatment plan should be. But with one of them working for the other side, it will never happen. We'll need to go with a third, neutral party to get you on medication."

Jeremy groaned. "No more interviews."

"There may be more, should you receive treatment. The doctor would need to follow up and make sure there's progress."

"Okay, let's just do it."

"I can arrange that." Linda wrote a reminder to herself. "We need to start preparing you for these public appearances, since the camera will be allowed in the courtroom. I'll arrange for you to get a haircut before the next hearing. The public views you as a villain. We need to show them you're still a human, just in need of help."

"Okay, if you say so," Jeremy said, not pleased. Everything felt like it was spiraling out of control. He knew it wouldn't be a quick process, but two years was a long time to stay in the same solitary cell. The plan was to keep him in the county detention center for the duration of the trial. He couldn't legally be sent to a prison unless sentenced, and the center was only a five minute drive to the courthouse.

He wanted desperately to tell Linda about his experiment, but had no idea how she would react. The risk outweighed the reward.

At least the doctor had given him a diagnosis they could work with.

Psychosis does open the door to a lot of possibilities. Dr. Brown may have spared my life. Am I really suffering from something, or did I do a good job of selling it?

Jeremy pondered this as he returned to his cell, certain he had no mental issues.

* * *

The following week, a state-appointed doctor paid a visit to Jeremy. Dr. Chang was a young psychiatrist in his mid-thirties who had just come to the U.S. from his home in South Korea. He had a full head of thick black hair slicked to the side, and high cheekbones that complemented his youthful appearance. Jeremy had a round of interviews with Dr. Chang, whose sole purpose was to implement a medication plan for the inmate.

The interview with Dr. Chang only lasted three hours in total, much shorter than the marathons Jeremy had grown accustomed to with Dr. Reed and Dr. Brown. Dr. Chang's questions weren't focused on his childhood or his inner desires, but rather his medical history. Heavy duty drugs would be administered as long as Jeremy passed as healthy enough to receive them. The doctor took urine and blood samples, as well as scraped Jeremy's skin with various swabs to check for allergic reactions.

Dr. Chang returned the next day with a plan.

"Mr. Heston, I'm prescribing you Chlorpromazine. We'll be starting with small dosages every other day, to make sure there are no major side effects. It will make you feel drowsy. You need to report immediately if you feel any sort of chest tightness or severe muscle spasms. These occurrences are extremely rare, but be aware. Once we're in the clear, I'll increase your dose."

Jeremy started taking Chlorpromazine that same day. The pills gave him a high that reminded him of his college days, smoking marijuana in his dorm room. A half hour after he swallowed the pill, his body relaxed to the point where he could barely stand up from his cot. His mind drifted into the clouds and he felt as if his soul had actually risen from his body and was looking down on him.

The days in between doses were to protect him from developing an addiction to the drugs. While he didn't seem to develop a physical dependence right away, his mind craved the high—it gave him something to look forward to every other day.

12

Chapter 12

Friday, September 19, 2016

Jeremy sat in court, a long day ahead. Both sides would debate what evidence would be allowed in the trial. He had grown a slight tolerance to his medication by now, but could still feel its subtle relaxation kick in after a few minutes. Pre-medication, he would have dreaded the long day in court, but with the medication it became bearable as he mostly zoned out for good chunks of the day.

He still wore his dark red uniform, but Linda assured him that he'd be able to wear a suit once the trial actually started. He'd also receive a fresh buzz cut for his scraggly hair. "The public is going to see you, and they'll see a different person. So far it's been mug shots and stills from the courtroom, when you weren't at your best. Come trial time, you'll look like an upstanding citizen."

Everything had gone according to Linda's plan so far.

Geoff Batchelor glared at them across the aisle before the judge entered the courtroom, silencing the soft murmurs from the gallery.

The judge's instructions from the last hearing were in effect: Media were sitting only in the back row of the gallery. The rest of the seats were filled with people whose lives Jeremy had ruined—and Jeremy's parents, who had a reserved seat in the front row, behind the defense table. Jeremy had avoided eye contact with them as he entered the room, but could feel their stare burning a hole in the back of his head. Every time he shuffled into the courtroom, dragging his shackles, he faced the gallery of people but refused to look at them. They were all blank faces as far as he was concerned. Linda had made it plenty clear that he should steer away from showing any outward emotion. And locking eyes with his mom or dad would surely break the composure he had formed.

The court sat in awkward silence, waiting for the judge to start the proceedings. "Good morning, everyone," Judge Zamora said, after flipping through documents on his bench. "We have a long day ahead of us, over a thousand pieces of evidence to review. This may even lead into tomorrow, so we won't waste any time with pleasantries. There will be no camera in court today, as this is merely a preliminary hearing to discuss evidence. The public doesn't need to know about evidence that will not be allowed in the trial. Mr. Batchelor, you may start us off."

The legal teams had come fully staffed for the hearing, groups of attorneys and assistants huddled around the tables and behind the bar. For the defense, the prior hearings had just been Linda and Wilbert along with a young woman he guessed to be an intern who sat behind the attorneys, taking notes and whispering to Wilbert at random times. Today, however, another man sat beside Wilbert, and there were three others who joined the intern, each with thick notepads and pens that moved quickly whenever a word was spoken. No one ever spoke to Jeremy aside from Linda, and he supposed this was done on purpose. She was his direct representation, while everyone else was on her team to help.

Across the aisle, Geoff and a female attorney whispered to each other as she flipped through a folder of documents before he proceeded to the podium facing Judge Zamora.

Geoff and his team would end up doing most of the speaking for the day. They had mountains of evidence to present, while Jeremy's defense team just had the interviews with Dr. Brown, and some other minor details.

For Jeremy, the evidence presented throughout the day caused ups and downs. Then there were stretches of time filled with complete boredom, as they submitted each individual bullet casing, shards of drywall, computers, and video footage of his interviews with Dr. Reed.

Other times, the presentations occupied all of Jeremy's attention and poked at his soul. The crime scene photos were enlarged on the screen, showing every detail of the bullet wounds, blood trails, and dead bodies. Jeremy's stomach churned, seeing the graphic pictures. Faces of people he'd known for years, busted open, blood and brains spilling out. Each victim had at least thirty pictures that fully captured their violent demise.

Each victim was identified by name, sending a wave of sorrow throughout Jeremy. He knew this part would be difficult, even back when he was planning, but still experienced plenty of remorse.

The prosecution presented the pictures of Sylvia last of the thirteen victims. Her face rested peacefully, her eyes closed by Jeremy before the police had arrived. A hole opened in the flesh on her throat reminded Jeremy of a broken egg after a chick hatches. He wondered what was going through Sylvia's mind before that bullet cut off her esophagus. *She must have been so confused to see me behind that gun. Rest in peace, my friend, I'm sorry.*

Jeremy slumped in his chair at the sight of the picture, and Linda nudged him to sit up before anyone else noticed.

The pictures of the training room grabbed Jeremy's full attention. On the day of the shooting, as meticulously as he'd planned, he hadn't expected a room full of sales reps in the training room and had been surprised upon finding them there. His time had been running out when he'd entered the room, so he'd opened fire without staying to see the damage he left behind.

The pictures presented showed more gore. Since everyone had hidden under their desks, the walls remained a pristine white. The blue carpeting, however, had turned purple from all the blood soaking in it. Three dead bodies appeared in the pictures, with streaks of blood leading toward the doors where others had presumably crawled to safety.

He remembered the feeling of his rifle: hot to the touch. It would probably have jammed had he tried to shoot any more after the training room.

Jeremy had walked out of the training room to a silent office. Other than the faint humming of computers, all he could hear was the sound of his own breathing and his heart pounding in his ears. Bloody footsteps had trailed around the corner toward the H.R. department and presumably out the front door.

When Jeremy had returned to his side of the office, with a quarter of his coworkers dead on the ground and the rest having fled while he had a ball in the training room, he'd sat at his desk and dropped his rifle with an echoing clatter. He felt totally alone in the world, knowing there was now no going back, no way to escape his actions.

He had felt at peace with it, though. Despite the doubts and fears that had built up before the big day, once the act was complete he knew he'd done the right thing. There were thousands of people suffering from the same loneliness as him, trapped in their own mind with no escape.

He was the only hope his fellow trapped souls had, to get them out of the dark, to get them the help they needed to live a normal life.

No matter what anyone says, I did this for all of us.

Jeremy snapped out of his memories when he heard Jamie's name mentioned. Linda was arguing with Geoff about her validity as a witness.

"Ms. Sylvester had nothing to do with this crime. She and the defendant had ended their relationship seven months before the incident. She has no relevance to this case."

"Your Honor," Geoff cut in. "In cases like this, there are life events that lead up to such a heinous crime. I think an interview with Ms. Sylvester may give us some insight as to how the relationship ended, and if that had any effect on the defendant's behavior. She might have even noticed a change in his mental health that could be beneficial to the defense."

Judge Zamora stared at Geoff, his fist propped at his mouth, weighing his decision. "I'm going to disallow Ms. Sylvester as a witness. There are surely numerous outside factors that influenced the defendant's actions, but this one simply doesn't fit with the timeline."

Geoff sat down, pissed off.

Jamie.

Jeremy hadn't thought much about Jamie during his time in jail, too consumed with the horrific images from March 11 in his mind every time he closed his eyes. He had loved her. At one time he believed he would marry her. He closed his eyes and remembered her scent.

What had she thought, seeing his face in the news? She was probably devastated and relieved, he guessed: devastated to think she had dated a mass murderer, relieved to have ended the relationship before things went so terribly wrong.

Did our breakup lead to me doing this?

He thought back to that time. His life had been crumbling all around him. He had been rejected for a promotion for a second time by Shelly. That was what had really ignited the spark. Shelly. She had fucked him over more times than he could count. The thought of her still made his blood boil, and he wondered if she was haunting his mind from the grave.

If Jamie hadn't called off the relationship, would things have gone differently? Jeremy couldn't know for sure. He sat in court today for killing thirteen people and wounding twenty-two others. That was the only truth he knew for sure.

As the day progressed, more memories flooded his mind as names were mentioned: Clark, Dr. Siva, Nicole. He would be seeing all of these people at some point in the near future and they would testify about what happened that day and the days leading up to it.

But Jeremy had covered his tracks. There had still been no evidence of premeditation.

* * *

By the end of the day, at 4 p.m., Jeremy was emotionally drained. The medication kept him relaxed enough to not let his emotions get the best of him. More than a thousand exhibits of evidence had been officially submitted, along with 112 witnesses. Judge Zamora acted quickly and confidently on every decision, hurrying the attorneys through the process.

"Your Honor, the defense would like to motion for a continuance. We haven't fully reviewed the video interviews between Mr. Heston and the two psychiatrists."

"How much more time do you think you'll need?" the judge asked.

"I'd say two months."

"Mr. Batchelor?"

"Two months is good, Your Honor," Geoff said. His team hadn't reviewed all fifty hours of footage either.

"Very well," the judge said. "We can plan for a hearing on the 21st of November. Thank you all for your speedy work today. Court is adjourned." Judge Zamora banged his gavel and disappeared to his chambers.

"Today was a good day," Linda told Jeremy before the officer came to take him back to jail. "We had a lot of things go our way."

Jeremy nodded. Linda had told him to refrain from speaking in the courtroom unless directly addressed by the judge. The defense team was there to speak on his behalf.

Jeremy stood when the officer arrived and glanced over his shoulder, to see his father staring at him, and his mother crying beside him.

13

Chapter 13

Monday, November 21, 2016

A light snow fell over the courthouse as the trial inched closer toward an official start. Jeremy had continued his routine of popping pills and becoming a vegetable on his cot every other day. The days between medication bored him. They brought him books to read, but he couldn't make his mind focus. Jail had managed to turn his once brilliant mind into a pile of useless mush in his skull. A day in court was just the change of pace he needed.

"Your Honor, we have new exhibits we'd like to submit for evidence," Geoff Batchelor said.

Both parties had officially agreed on the submission of the videos in full, which was supposed to have been the topic of the hearing.

Linda sat up stiffly. The district attorney's office had emailed a memo that morning with information on the new exhibit, she had told Jeremy. Geoff Batchelor wanted to play dirty.

Geoff saw the disgust on her face and addressed it. "My apologies, counsel, there are some things we came across late yesterday."

"Proceed," Judge Zamora said sternly.

"Your Honor, we would like to present exhibit 1672." Geoff held up a manila envelope. "The contents are from the defendant's former employer. We have a form that shows the defendant was placed on what they called a PIP, or 'performance improvement plan' three months before his attack. There is also documentation that the defendant was denied a raise, along with paperwork showing the pending termination of his employment—set for March 11, 2016."

Someone in the back gasped. Linda scribbled on her notepad, her hand shaking. She bolted up from her seat.

"Your Honor, we need time to review these new documents," she said. Jeremy could hear the anger in her voice.

"Mr. Batchelor, how many pages are your documents?" Judge Zamora asked.

Geoff flipped through the envelope, as if he didn't already know the answer. "Looks like five pages."

"Ms. Kennedy, we will get you copies of these documents to review today," Judge Zamora said. "We'll take a recess and reconvene after lunch. That should be enough time for you to review. Is there anything else, Mr. Batchelor?"

"Yes, Your Honor. We would like to submit Richard Heston as a witness."

Uncle Ricky.

"A relative of the defendant?" the judge questioned.

"Yes, Your Honor. The defendant's uncle. It is our understanding that the defendant and his uncle spent time together at shooting ranges over the years, and we would like to hear from him regarding just that."

Jeremy's heart dropped to the bottom of his gut. Linda peered at Jeremy with a look of disgust. He could read her mind: why the hell hadn't he mentioned any of this to her? She knew an objection would do no good. If Jeremy's uncle had directly been involved with guns of any sort, there was no way around it.

"We accept the witness, Your Honor," Linda said, defeated. Geoff smirked.

"Very well. Let's break for recess and plan to meet back here at 2 p.m." Judge Zamora banged his gavel and left.

Linda conversed briefly with Wilbert to her left before returning to her notebook and speaking to Jeremy under her breath. "It would be helpful to know these kind of things ahead of time. If you were about to get fired, this looks pretty bad for you."

Jeremy nodded, mind racing. There had to be a way out. The PIP had ended a good month before the shooting, and his relationship with Shelly and Mark had improved from that point on. The stiffed raise could easily be explained as a result of the PIP. *I was never told I was being fired, only that it was being considered. The only people in the room that day were Shelly and Mark. And me.* He smirked. Only one of them was still above ground, and that person would not be testifying. *Fuck you, Shelly, looks like you won't be able to do any more damage to my life. It's my word against yours, and neither of us are going to say a damn thing.*

It would all depend on what kind of notes Shelly had left with H.R. If she'd simply filed the paperwork for his termination, that didn't prove Jeremy had been informed the firing was coming. Jeremy had spent enough time in court by now, he'd started to think like a lawyer, looking for loopholes.

As far as his Uncle Ricky, Jeremy hadn't heard from him in quite some time, despite having visited his cabin every weekend for shooting practice.

* * *

"Why would you not mention this?" Linda demanded through the glass divider. She had come to see Jeremy in prison right after the hearing. Her team had read through the documents provided by Open Hands regarding Jeremy's crumbling work performance, and had filed an objection, which was denied as expected. The documents were official evidence now.

"That all seemed so petty, in the past. I didn't think it was relevant, and I still don't."

Linda shook her head. "You were going to be fired on the day you murdered half your department—how on Earth could that be irrelevant?" She had never raised her voice to Jeremy, and her passion aroused him. "They're building a premeditation case around this."

"I had no idea I was getting fired." Jeremy decided to go all-in on his bluff, hoping Shelly had failed to mention in her notes that she had warned Jeremy about being fired. It was Thursday, March 10, when she had pulled him into the conference room to rant about the bullying he had supposedly done toward Janae. Mark had sat in the corner silently as Shelly told Jeremy she was considering firing him. Shelly was so emotional that day, she could have easily let that detail slip in her write-up. Since Linda didn't dispute his claim that he didn't know—and she had read the documents—he assumed he was right.

"We'll come back to the firing. You didn't receive a raise that year, after having received at least a ten percent raise the prior three years. How can you expect the jurors to not see the shootings as you getting some sort of revenge?"

"It's a new company. They bought us and did things different.

I wasn't the only to not get a raise."

Linda took notes as Jeremy spoke. "And then this performance improvement plan in January? The prosecution is probably going to pin that as your turning point, the time you decided enough is enough."

"The plan also mentioned how Shelly offered me a severance package if I wanted to leave, did it not?"

"Yes, it did."

"Why wouldn't I have just taken the money? It was a nice amount."

Linda didn't respond, only stared at Jeremy through the glass.

"I was happy there. It was an amazing company to work for. I had no intention of leaving. All I ever wanted, toward the end, was to get out from under Shelly's supervision, to somewhere I would be appreciated."

"Why did you shoot Shelly first?"

Jeremy jolted back and tossed his hands in the air. "I told you, I don't remember the shooting. I know I walked in the building and down the hallway to our department. Shelly's desk was first when you entered from the side door, that's probably why I shot her first."

Linda stared at him, not blinking—and from what Jeremy could tell, not breathing either.

"Something's off, and I don't like it. You're obviously a smart kid, about to graduate with a degree in psychology and scheduled to begin a master's program in the fall. I personally have a hard time believing an event like this wouldn't be planned out in great detail, especially considering how smoothly it went for you. And that leads me to believe that you planned this out, that you knew exactly how to cover your tracks. You understand the psychology side of the matter, that's a given, but how did you know how to cover it up legally? You have no background whatsoever with the law—surely you would have missed a detail somewhere along the line." Linda appeared calm, but Jeremy could tell from her voice that she was upset. *Whose side are you on? Why are you trying to poke so many holes in my story?*

"Who are we calling as witnesses?" Jeremy asked. The last hearing about the evidence was a whole lot of the prosecution talking while Linda sat there taking notes.

"We only have one witness: Dr. Brown."

"That's it?"

"That's all there is. Everyone that was tied to your life before the shooting has been called by the prosecution. Don't worry, though, Dr. Brown is going to provide some valuable insight that we can work with."

"It seems weird for them to have over 100 witnesses and we only have one person?"

"I understand your concern, but there really are no other options. We could've asked your parents to testify, but the jury would just see that as a bias ploy. Besides, we'll need them to testify on your behalf should the verdict come back as guilty. Then we can have them create some sort of sympathy for you, to spare your life in the sentencing phase."

Spare my life?

"I don't understand why I can't testify," Jeremy asked, something that had been on his mind for the past couple days. "This is my trial. Why can't I defend myself?"

"Jeremy." Linda replied, clearly trying to hold her composure. "This is a fragile case, we can't afford to take any gambles. Geoff Batchelor would eat you alive on the witness stand. I've seen him do it. Five minutes with him will get you the needle quicker than you know."

"I'm not afraid of him."

"It's not about fear. I'm sure you could debate him on the principles of psychology and win, but this is the courtroom—his home turf. He has years of experience. He'll bait you into saying things you don't want to say, make your story fuzzy. All he has to do is plant a little doubt in the jury's minds and you lose. Dr. Brown is your best chance of getting out of this alive."

Dr. Brown was an intense woman, and Geoff's intimidation tactics wouldn't work on her. She was also "by the book" and would stick to the facts. This would be Dr. Brown's fifty-fifth trial serving as an expert witness, so she had plenty of experience on the witness stand.

Jeremy sat in silence. He wanted to tell her everything: the meetings with Dr. Siva asking him how he could change the world, Shelly and Mark fucking with his career, his decision to change the world at their expense.

But he couldn't. She'd never believe it, and if she did, having that knowledge could throw a wrench in everything she had done so far to prepare for the trial. *Can't take any gambles.* She could easily drop him as a client after learning of his twisted plans, leaving him back at square one, with no attorney wanting to work with him. If the news spread that he had knowingly done his crime in the name of science, any chance of a stay at an asylum would go out the door.

"You're right, Linda. I'm sorry," he said, lowering his eyes. "You know what you're doing. I'll do whatever you think is best."

"Thank you." She sat back in her chair and let out a deep exhale. "I still feel that something is not adding up in your story."

"I think you're giving me too much credit."

"You've conveniently forgotten anything that had to do with the shooting. You remember walking into the office, but not opening fire?"

Why the fuck *did I say that?* He wished he could go back to his first meeting with her and start again. He had been caught off guard when she showed up, instead expecting to see the nervous public defender the court had assigned to him.

"Why did you buy an AR-15 as your first firearm purchase?"

He decided to leave Ricky out of it. If Ricky wanted to admit being the one who introduced Jeremy to the weapon, then that would be his choice. "I'd shot one at the range and loved it. Wanted one of my own." He assessed her reaction; she didn't believe him. "I thought you were on my side. What's with the attack?"

"*Attack?* Don't you know what's coming? The district attorney is going to *attack* your very existence. He's going to make you out to be a monster, as scum of the Earth. *I'm* trying to make sure you don't get sentenced to death. Don't you ever question whose side I'm on. You better think long and hard about telling me the truth. If not, well—it's your ass."

Linda hung up her phone and stood. "I'll see you tomorrow," she shouted as she stormed out of the visitation room, inmates and their visitors staring at her, and then at Jeremy.

He hung up the phone slowly before the officer arrived to take him back to his cell. *I need to tell her.*

14

Chapter 14

Tuesday, December 6, 2016

Across the country, Ricky Heston sat with his feet in the sand, at a private resort in West Palm Beach, Florida. When the news broke about Jeremy, he wanted to get as far away as possible, unable to come to terms with what his nephew had done. His brother had changed irreparably, as a result of Jeremy's actions. Speaking with Robert was like talking with a depressed teenager: one-word answers and shoulder shrugs.

Ricky had originally escaped to his cabin a couple weeks after Jeremy's shooting. Getting into nature always brought him back to his senses. Snow had dumped in the mountains the weekend of the shooting, leaving him to wait it out and allow some of it to melt before making the drive.

When Ricky parked his car in front of the cabin and stepped out, gravel crunching beneath his shoes, across the patches of snow spread across his driveway he noticed a gleaming light lodged in the muddy ground.

He approached and bent down to pick up the hollow gold casing. He knew what it was right away. "Fuck," he said. The news reports had given great detail about the type of gun and ammunition Jeremy had used in his rampage, and the empty shell casing in his fingers was an exact match.

He rolled the cold metal between his forefinger and thumb, then stuffed the shell into his jeans pocket and hurried toward the trees in the distance.

Examining the surface of the bark, the words "Jesus Christ" fell out of his mouth. At least a dozen holes spread across the surface of the tree, and they all matched the caliber of bullet Jeremy had used.

He didn't even bother entering his cabin before jumping back into his truck and returning to the highway. His mind raced as he drove faster and faster, wanting to put some distance between himself and the cabin.

"What the fuck, Jeremy?" he shouted in his truck. "Why the fuck did you drag me into this?"

Ricky felt his mind spiraling, creating wicked thoughts of being arrested as an accomplice. If the police had found what he'd just found, Ricky would have a lot of explaining to do. And yet he'd had no idea what had occurred on his property.

"It doesn't have to be Jeremy. It could have been anyone. Someone from the Wells cabin. They shoot AR's." He tried to assure himself that everything was fine. "Who am I kidding? This is Jeremy's shell, and those are his bullet holes."

I need to get rid of it. Get it as far away as possible.

He stayed on the freeway, passing Denver and continuing toward Denver International Airport. He had frequent flyer points thanks to his travel for work, and he could work remotely. He'd already had his suitcase packed in anticipation of a week's stay at the cabin.

When he arrived at the airport he stuffed the empty shell in his suitcase, planning to check the bag to get it through security and onto the plane. A flight was departing in two hours to Fort Lauderdale, so he rushed to the airline counter to buy a one-way ticket and check his bag. Everything went smoothly despite the panic surging through his veins.

What would happen if they pulled his bag and searched it? If they found an empty bullet casing with Jeremy Heston's fingerprints on it, his life could completely flip. How would he explain himself?

Despite his disgust toward Jeremy, his natural reaction was to protect his nephew. He decided that he wouldn't tell the police that Jeremy had gone to his cabin. He wouldn't tell them about the holes in the trees. And he certainly wouldn't mention the empty shell.

If Ricky were questioned about anything, he would tell the truth: he hadn't seen or spoken to Jeremy in a few months, and he was as shocked as anyone when he saw the news.

Ricky waited for night and chucked the shell as far as he could into the moon's massive reflection in the blacked-out sea. He stood still for several minutes, the waves whooshing at his feet.

* * *

Ricky saw no urgent reason to return home.

Florida was fun. He was able to work from the beach after setting up a wireless hot spot through his cell phone. Watching beautiful twenty-somethings in bikinis made the days a little better. There were even women his age, in much better shape than himself. Maybe he would even start exercising and pursue one of them.

A Colorado native, Ricky missed the snow. It was December and snow would surely be falling soon if it hadn't already. If Jeremy hadn't poisoned his cabin with evidence, Ricky would probably be there, happily trapped by a foot of snow, doing nothing but drinking whiskey and listening to a Sinatra record.

Instead, Ricky was soaking in the rays on a cloudless eighty-degree day. His phone rang: a 303 area code, Denver.

"Hello?" He'd had a couple of piña coladas and tried to sound his sharpest.

"Hello, Mr. Heston, my name is Geoff Batchelor, district attorney for the eighteenth judicial district of Colorado."

Holy shit, Ricky thought, and dropped his empty glass into the sand. He recognized the name. He'd kept an eye on the trial online and knew Geoff Batchelor was the intimidating blond prosecuting attorney.

"Hello, Mr. Batchelor. What can I do for you?" Alcohol mixed with fear in Ricky's belly.

"I was hoping you might be able to stop in for questioning about your nephew, Jeremy. It's been brought to our attention that you and he used to frequent the shooting range."

"I'm actually in Florida for work."

Dead air filled the phone line, and Ricky checked his cell to make sure the call was still connected.

"That's okay, Mr. Heston. If you have time right now, we can record our conversation so that your statement may be used in court. Just be aware that you'll be asked to show up to the trial in person once it begins."

God damn it, Jeremy.

"Yes, of course. What sort of questions did you have for me?"

"When was the last time you saw your nephew?"

Ricky flipped through his mental calendar, thinking back to

their day at the shooting range. "I think it's been a little over a year now. I haven't heard from him since then."

"How often would you and he go to the shooting range?"

"The shooting range specifically, not too many times. Maybe a couple times a year. Most of the time we would go golfing, or to Nuggets and Broncos games. We always watched sports together."

Ricky caught himself speaking of Jeremy in the past tense and the thought pierced his heart.

"I see, and during your visits to the shooting range did he ever use an AR-15?"

"No." That was the truth. It was an M-16 that Ricky had let him use, which likely led to Jeremy's interest in an AR-15.

"Is there anything else you might like to inform us about that pertains to this case?"

Ricky felt his heart pounding in his head. *He knows nothing about the cabin, hasn't even mentioned the cabin.*

"No, sir, I don't believe so. Like I said, I haven't heard from Jeremy in a long time. I was as shocked as anyone when I saw the news."

"Fair enough. Please stay near your phone, my office may be in touch with more questions, and we'll also let you know when you'll be expected to appear in court. Thanks for your time today and enjoy the sunshine—we're getting a dumping of snow tonight."

Thanks, dick.

"Sounds good, Mr. Batchelor, please let me know how I can help."

They hung up and Ricky's heart continued to pulse in rapid bursts. It reminded him of the Edgar Allen Poe story "The Tell-Tale Heart," when the guilty man keeps hearing the heartbeat of his buried victim underneath his floor.

"You're okay. They didn't ask about the cabin. They may not even know about the cabin. You're okay." Two high school boys gawked at Ricky as he spoke to himself.

"Go back to school," he barked at them, and they shuffled away.

Guess I'm going home sooner than planned.

15

Chapter 15

Monday, December 12, 2016

With all evidence submitted and approved, the judge set a date of July 17, 2017 for the trial to begin. With a set date, it was now time to prepare for a plea bargain. When Linda took on the case, she believed getting Jeremy a life sentence to be the best possible outcome. As time progressed and more money was thrown into the trial by his parents, she had talked herself into a realistic possibility of getting Jeremy a 'not guilty by reason of insanity' verdict.

Linda had stressed over this day, anxious about how the district attorney would react. If Batchelor accepted the guilty plea in exchange for life in prison, they would have achieved her original best possible outcome. How realistic was an insanity plea?

While there were holes to fill in the insanity narrative, she still couldn't find a single detail that pointed to Jeremy planning out his slaughter. She knew she should just believe his claim that he had blacked out the night prior and the day of the shooting, but she still suspected something bigger was at play, and Jeremy was hiding it.

He had to have planned everything, she was convinced—but she decided to keep her mouth shut about it going forward. He was her client: she was paid to protect him, not persecute him.

"Batchelor won't accept the plea. There's not a chance," Wilbert told her. They met in her office before driving to the courthouse. "Then we can move on and prepare for trial."

They left the office and drove together in Linda's BMW, not speaking one word to each other. They both knew that the decision made at today's hearing would drastically affect the next several months of their lives.

Jeremy still gave her the creeps when they met, so she wouldn't be opposed to it all ending now, yet she sensed the universe had a different plan in mind.

They entered the courtroom to find Geoff reading over some papers. He looked up at them as they sat at their table. "Good morning, Linda. Wilbert."

"Morning, Governor," Linda replied without looking at the district attorney. She could tell from his voice that he had no plan to accept the plea. This case was just something to hang his future campaign on. Every day she saw him she hated him a little more.

A handful of cameras snapped behind Linda, and she looked up to see Jeremy entering the courtroom, dragging his shackles, an officer close behind him. He appeared dazed, likely high off his ass from the pills they had prescribed. Jeremy nodded at her and Wilbert as he sat down, not saying a word.

"All rise!" the bailiff called from the corner of the room as Judge Zamora entered with his black cloak flowing behind him.

"Good morning, folks. Today should be quick. The defense team will offer a plea bargain should they choose. We'll discuss some clerical matters, and then we'll reconvene tomorrow morning for the prosecution's decision on the plea bargain."

"Your Honor, we have one final piece of evidence to submit. We sent it to the defense yesterday as well," Geoff said.

"Okay, what is it?"

"Exhibit 1972. These are copies of the 911 calls made the morning of March 11, from within the office building where the crime occurred."

"Ms. Kennedy?" the judge asked.

"No objections, Your Honor." The calls made to dispatch were standard evidence.

"Perfect. Thank you." The judge paused while he made a note.

"Okay. Ms. Kennedy, will your team exercise a plea bargain today?"

"Yes, Your Honor. We offer to plead guilty to the charges in exchange for a lifetime prison sentence."

Jeremy cringed at the words and his legs started to bounce underneath the table. He looked in Geoff's direction to read his reaction, but there was none: the D.A. was taking notes of his own, with an expressionless face.

"Mr. Batchelor, you will have an answer for us tomorrow regarding the defense team's offer."

The judge proceeded to discuss questions that had arisen regarding some exhibits of evidence, before adjourning for the day.

* * *

December 13, 2016

Jeremy didn't have his pills on a day he wished he did. His entire experiment could be flushed down the toilet this morning, and his body shivered nervously in anticipation of the decision. The courtroom felt warmer than usual, and the tension in the air was thick enough to cut with a knife. Those in attendance were quieter than they had been the previous days.

Linda noticed her client rocking beside her and whispered under her breath, "We're okay."

Jeremy had no way of knowing if she said this because of a gut feeling or if she actually knew something. She had assured him the day before that the plea bargain was simply a posturing move to give the district attorney some additional paperwork to do, and to potentially stall the start of the trial. "I can say with certainty he will not accept the offer," she had told him.

Still, Jeremy sat at the defense table, guts bubbling in anticipation. *There's no such thing as a sure thing. He could accept the offer and this all ends today. Off to prison I go.*

Judge Zamora entered the courtroom. "Good morning. Mr. Batchelor, does the prosecution accept the plea bargain offered by the defense?"

Geoff rose from his seat and buttoned his suit before speaking. "Your Honor, the prosecution declines the plea bargain."

The tension left Jeremy's shoulders in an instant and he could sense the same from Linda.

"We believe Ms. Kennedy simply made the offer to delay the start of trial. We absolutely do not accept the plea."

Linda shook her head.

"Mr. Batchelor, does this mean that you will pursue the death penalty?"

"Yes, Your Honor, we intend to pursue the death penalty for this case," Geoff said without hesitation. The words had less of a punch than Jeremy expected, partly because he knew they were coming.

"Very well. Ms. Kennedy, since the prosecution has rejected your offer, would you like to make any changes to your plea?"

"Yes, Your Honor. We will now plead 'not guilty by reason of insanity'."

Judge Zamora jotted a note. "Very well," he said. "Ladies and gentlemen, with this plea please be reminded that it now becomes the prosecution's burden to prove beyond a reasonable doubt that the defendant was sane during the time of the crime. Mr. Batchelor, do you understand?"

"Yes, Your Honor."

Judge Zamora flipped through a calendar on his bench. "Let's aim for July 17 for opening statements. Which means jury selection should begin on the 10th of April. Are there any questions?"

"Your Honor, I would like to request a continuance. We still have hundreds of documents to go through." Linda spoke confidently, as if she expected the continuance to be granted.

"Ms. Kennedy, I don't want to push this trial out any further. Are you telling me you won't be ready in time?"

"Not in time for jury selection in April. We would need all of our research complete to be in any position to discuss jurors."

Judge Zamora pursed his lips. "Mr. Batchelor, any objection to the continuance?"

"No, Your Honor."

"Okay then," the judge said. "We will plan for jury selection to commence on July 17 instead, with the trial beginning on October 23. Please hold to these dates, as there will be no more delays granted. Court is adjourned."

"We're going to trial," Linda whispered to Jeremy before turning to Wilbert.

Jeremy's gut fluttered in excitement. He would be moving on to the next phase in his experiment.

* * *

December 14, 2016

"There are three possible verdicts now: guilty, not guilty, and not guilty by reason of insanity." Linda had come to visit Jeremy the next day and fill him in on the next steps. "We can eliminate 'not guilty' as a possibility. That would allow you to walk home a free man. 'Not guilty by reason of insanity' is what we're aiming for. This will allow your sentence to be to a mental institution for an amount of time determined by the judge. A 'guilty' verdict would have the trial move to a sentencing phase where the jury will decide if you should receive life in prison or lethal injection.

"Our plan is to focus on two things: a lack of premeditation, and a narrative. Premeditation is what throws the insanity defense out the door, but so far there's no proof to suggest it. As far as a narrative, this is where Wilbert will be helping the most. We're going to take your interview with Dr. Brown and create a story that highlights a troubled past. We need the jury to think you've always been mentally unwell and never received help."

"But I haven't always been this way. Isn't that just as

meaningful?"

"I know that. And no. Juries don't buy that people can randomly snap one day. They want to hear about a buildup to it, and that's what we'll give them. We're working with a jury psychologist who specializes in these kind of things, and he agrees with our approach. We're going to focus heavily on your great-grandfather and drill that into the jury's head every chance we can."

Jeremy flashed back to his notebook. If that notebook were to turn up, his life would be over. But the notebook was surely buried at the bottom of a landfill, after he tossed it in a gas station trash can.

That notebook contained the only evidence of premeditation. He wished he had burned it.

Chapter 16

Monday, January 23, 2017

Now that Linda had until July to be fully prepared for the trial, she didn't want to overlook a single detail. In their war room at the office, on a long white board running the length of the conference room, Linda drew out a timeline of events on the board, to anticipate what the opposition would focus on.

Wilbert said, "If they want to prove premeditation, they'll need to focus on the months before the shooting. The PIP in January will be key, as well as the job rejection in October. Also, the hiring of Mark Fernandez after Jeremy's rejection."

Linda circled each event as Wilbert mentioned it, and took a step back to examine.

"So we'll need testimony from those close to Jeremy at those times. Based on preliminary interviews, I think his friend at the office, Clark, will give us some good insight into how Jeremy was acting, as well as his professor, Dr. Adrian Siva. What should we do about those events right before the shooting? The firing and the raise."

"The raise is nothing. I looked into it, and Jeremy was right, quite a few people were not given raises. There is also no documentation that he was warned of a firing. It appears as if Shelly Williams drew up his termination without even a discussion with H.R. Her mind was made up to get rid of Jeremy on March 11. It may sound farfetched, but it appears to be a coincidence."

"But Geoff is going to make these exact events into Jeremy's motive," Linda said.

Wilbert replied, "He has no motive—he's insane! His illness has always been with him, dormant and waiting. These events merely woke it up and he acted out in rage. Dr. Brown even confirmed this."

"I don't think that's good enough to get him off."

"Get him off?" Wilbert teased. "On the insanity defense? Linda, our priority is to keep him off death row. Anything better than that is icing on the cake. He'll end up with our original plea bargain if all goes well in the trial. You don't actually think he's going to be sent to a mental institution, do you?"

"Well, yes. There are no signs of premeditation."

"Linda. We've both been in this business a long time. We both know that jurors make decisions based on facts. They're not going to try to get into the mind of the defendant and create compassion for him. A jury is going to see a man who was rejected for two promotions, placed on disciplinary action, stiffed a raise, and was about to be fired—all by the same woman, who he shot first, by the way, on the day he was to be fired."

"We have Dr. Brown to testify about his illness."

"Jurors don't care about science. DNA evidence is as far as their understanding goes, and that's not what's being discussed here. This is a trial where the defendant is guilty of the crime."

"You're the one who told me we had a chance, with all the money the family is throwing at the case." Wilbert's intensity was starting to wear on Linda. As he was her boss, and the head of the firm, she couldn't call him out on it. And as she knew from experience, a defense team needed to be united going into a trial. When everyone was just angling for their own agenda, the defendant suffered as a result.

"And we do have a chance, but I'm also a realist. Even with unlimited funds this is still an uphill battle. Only two percent of insanity pleas win. Having money increases those chances to maybe five. I love the confidence, but you need to set your target to something more achievable. Geoff is going to tell a long story about how Jeremy became so fed up with life that he snapped, and took it out on everyone who wronged him. What we should be focused on is creating our own story, of how Jeremy led a normal life like anyone else before caving to the symptoms of his illness. Make the jury and the public relate to him. The more they feel connected to him, the less likely they'll send him to his death."

Death penalty cases, Linda knew, had a way of causing their attorneys more stress than normal. They were going to need to take a lot of deep breaths between now and July.

17

Chapter 17

Monday, July 10, 2017

The months since January fell into a routine for Jeremy. Less hearings were scheduled, leaving him in his lonely cell to think about life. He acknowledged his failing mind and requested crossword and Sudoku puzzles to help sharpen his ability to think.

The officers in the jail had grown more lax towards Jeremy. They still hated him, but showing their disgust required too much energy to maintain for over a year. When he had entered jail all those months ago, it was typical for an officer to mutter a hateful message to Jeremy when they dropped off his food. Now, they simply remained silent when dealing with him. *We're practically friends,* Jeremy thought and giggled to himself.

Even Linda had remained out of touch, having assured Jeremy she would catch him up on all of their progress when the time came. She had stopped by in June to inform Jeremy that a record nine thousand jury summons had been sent out to Denver area registered voters, the most in American history. Jury selection was the last hurdle to clear before the trial would begin. Jeremy was due in court every day for jury selection, a process they expected to take two to three months. Jeremy thought he might die of boredom at first, but appreciated it after two days in to the process.

Jeremy fell in love with lunch time in the courthouse. He sat in a small holding room near the judge's chambers, with two officers standing guard outside the door. The room had bare, white walls, a small square table, and a chair bolted into the ground. He only used the room during the court's lunch recess each day. He was allowed to roam around the room, no smaller than his cell, and enjoy the view from the window that overlooked a green field of tall grass. The jail had granted him one hour of outdoors time each week, but he'd often pass it up as going outside would require him to wear his shackles.

The cafeteria in the courthouse provided his lunch, a major upgrade from the pile of slop he had to force down every day in jail. He was given a turkey and ham sandwich, chips, and a bottle of water each day in court—nothing more, nothing less.

The sandwich filled his mouth with an explosion of flavors more tasty than anything he'd eaten since the spaghetti at his mom's house the night before the shooting. He savored every bite and treasured the time in the private room as his own. Once lunch was delivered, no one bothered him until it was time for court to resume.

Jury selection dragged from July into early October. The first month of questioning jurors was a learning process for Jeremy. He found the process to be fairly quick paced, several dozens of jurors receiving their dismissal each day. Both the prosecution and defense were allowed ten peremptory challenges, meaning they could choose ten people to dismiss without giving a reason. With a pool of 9,000 jurors, the ten challenges were all used up within the first day, practically meaningless in the grand scheme.

Both attorneys grilled the jurors with questions about their thoughts on guns, the death penalty, mental health, and any potential discrepancies they may have had in the workplace with managers or coworkers. As expected, most people shared their stories of missing out on raises and promotions, and some even offered to discuss why they hated their boss. These people were promptly dismissed.

After July, Jeremy felt like the jurors that came into the courtroom were all the same people on some sort of repetitive loop. Despite being so important, jury selection had to be the most boring aspect of a trial. Many jurors gawked at Jeremy when they entered the courtroom, seeing the mass murderer in the flesh. Most days he zoned out thanks to his pills, staring into space as his lawyers worked to find the best people to spare his life. Linda had requested another continuance in July and was promptly denied the request. October 23 was set in stone for opening statements.

"We're shooting for a three-to-one ratio of women to men on the jury, and so far we're on track," Linda explained to Jeremy one day after court. "Women are less likely to vote in favor of the death penalty compared to men."

Linda kept a thick folder with lists of juror numbers high-lighted either red, green, or yellow. Jeremy assumed this was her way of tracking the jurors and their answers, noting who they would want to select. Every week that passed seemed to add one or two more jurors to the twenty four they were looking to secure for the lengthy trial.

Jeremy returned to his cell every night with a twisting knot in his stomach. *I've been sitting in the same room with the people who will decide my fate.*

He rarely took the time to appreciate how small he was in the universe. The stars had to align perfectly if he were to get the verdict needed to continue his work. Everything had to fall in place from the judge, the attorneys, their staffs, the witnesses, and the jury. A criminal case like his had thousands of moving pieces that he would never even know about, but those pieces all had to fall in place for him to receive an insanity verdict.

18

Chapter 18

Monday, October 9, 2017

By the time October arrived, Linda had achieved a slightly better ratio than she had projected: nineteen of the twenty-four jurors were women. After the boring three months of jury selection, the courtroom once again buzzed with anticipation now that the jury was set.

Jeremy stared across the room at the crowded jury box, where twenty-four strangers would decide his fate. He studied them as they waited for the judge to begin speaking to the jury for their initial instructions. Of the women, half appeared to be over the age of fifty, while the rest were closer to Jeremy's age, in their late twenties. The five men seated were all middle-aged and had curious looks of anticipation on their faces.

The jury box was divided into three rows of eight. The front row and first half of the middle row were the actual twelve jurors. The second half of the middle row and the entire back row were the alternate jurors. It was common practice for a high-profile case and lengthy trial to have twelve alternates in case issues arose over time.

Some of these jurors look like they could croak any minute! Jeremy thought.

Judge Zamora spoke to the jury. "Thank you, folks, for committing to this trial. As you know, this is a high-profile case with national attention. The first and most important rule to remember is to not discuss the case with anyone, not even your significant others. There will be extensive media coverage of this trial. You are not to watch the news. If you find yourself in a situation where the trial comes up in conversation or on the TV, you must excuse yourself. I can't emphasize this enough.

"Also be aware that a camera will be in the courtroom, providing a live broadcast. You, the jurors, will not be shown on camera."

As Judge Zamora continued with his preliminary instructions for the jury, Jeremy looked the jury up and down, studying each of the main twelve. They each wore a name tag with big numbers written in black ink, identifying them by their juror number.

The first row of jurors were eight women. Jeremy studied them one by one, assigning a nickname to each based on a physical attribute.

Chubby, he thought for the woman in the first seat, clearly a regular at the buffet.

Snow White. An elderly woman with snow white hair.

Cakeface. One of the women his age, with a bit too much makeup on.

Broomstick. A younger woman with stiff blond hair.

Betty White. An elderly woman who looked tiny and gentle like the famous actress.

Ms. Serious. An older woman who wore glasses and a stone-faced expression, and glared at Jeremy.

89

Asian Girl. Another woman his age, with slanted eyes.

Rich Lady. A middle-aged woman with loads of jewelry on her neck, wrists, and fingers.

Jeremy moved his attention to the middle, where the first four seats rounded out the jury of twelve.

Lewis. An older black man with white curly hair, who reminded him of his old friend from the Bears.

Mr. CEO. A handsome middle-age man dressed in a sharp suit.

Lunch Lady. An older black woman who reminded Jeremy of his lunch lady in middle school.

Gamer Dude. A heavier man with scraggly hair and pimples spread across his face.

Each juror hung on to the judge's every word, except for Ms. Serious in the front row. She kept her head toward the judge, but Jeremy noticed her eyes wander around the courtroom before landing on him again.

Jeremy focused his attention on the woman. She stared at him from behind a pair of thin-framed glasses. She maintained a stern countenance, the corners of her mouth furled. He was pretty sure she wanted to jump across the room and strangle him. Her hair was a short, sandy brown with waves of gray.

Is she out to get me?

"Monday, October 23, will be the start of this trial. From that point forward I'll expect you all to be in your juror's room promptly at 8 a.m. every day. If you're running late, please contact the courtroom deputy, whom you'll meet before leaving today. Now, are there any questions from the jury?"

The jurors looked around at each other and no one spoke up.

"Questions from counsel?"

"No, Your Honor," Geoff said.

"Alright then, folks. I'll see you all back here on the 23rd for opening statements. Enjoy your two weeks until then." He banged his gavel and chatter filled the courtroom.

"Jeremy, please," a voice whispered from behind. He raised his head but didn't look back; he knew it was his mom. "Jeremy, we're coming to see you this week. We finally got permission." Her voice struck a painful chord in his chest.

When the officer arrived for Jeremy, he stood, turned back, and nodded to his mother before walking out of the room.

He thought about her during the short drive back to the jail. Dark gray clouds had formed in the sky and Jeremy ached for a chance to breathe fresh air as a free man. He hadn't been outdoors in a long time.

19

Chapter 19

Tuesday, October 10, 2017

Jeremy looked at his mother through the glass divider and saw how much she'd aged since the last time he'd really looked at her, at dinner the night before the shooting. Wrinkles, bags, and gray hair revealed themselves under the bright lights. She held the phone in a trembling hand and her eyes welled with tears, while Robert stood behind her with a hand on her back.

He had tossed and turned all night, anticipating what he would say to his parents after all this time. Nineteen months felt like an eternity, and it probably felt even longer for them. Their lives would have completely transformed while he sat in a cell and stared at a concrete wall, growing older but no wiser.

He had hundreds of questions he wanted to ask, but when he entered the visitation room and saw the lines on his mom's once youthful face, guilt took hold in his throat, making speech difficult. Memories clashed in his mind with thoughts of how the shooting had surely spun their lives down the shitter. Jeremy could see the pain swimming behind his parents' eyes.

"Oh, Jeremy," she gasped when he sat down and picked up

his phone. "What happened?"

All he could do was stare at her. Finally he managed to say, "Hi, Mom. Dad," tears forming in his eyes. He put an open palm up to the glass, wanting nothing more than to feel his mother's embrace.

"Are you okay?" she asked.

Tears rolled down his cheeks. "I'm fine. I need help, Mom. Linda's going to get me out of here, I just know it. I didn't want to do what I did."

Every thought of freedom flooded his mind. He hadn't seen his parents in over eighteen months, and all it took was five seconds to feel a wave of guilt and regret.

Her lips quivered and she broke into a heavy sob, handing the phone to Robert.

"Hi, son. It's been hard without you. I hope you're doing okay." His dad paused to contemplate his next words. "I told your mother this would be difficult." His words came out slurred. He was a man of few emotions, but Jeremy assumed he was fighting back tears of his own.

"I love you both. I'm so sorry," Jeremy said.

"We love you. I think we need to leave now. We'll try to come back another time."

Robert hung up the phone, squeezed his wife, and helped her out of the visitation room while she sobbed, seeming to hyperventilate.

Jeremy had never seen his father so defeated. So broken. The guilt he felt was the worst it had been since he had entered jail. All along he had been committed to the experiment, but he'd lost sight of how it would affect those closest to him. He wiped the tears from his face before returning to his cell for the evening.

* * *

The weeks leading up to the trial were eventful for Jeremy. He had appointments with barbers and suit tailors. He hadn't worn a suit since his interview with Open Hands almost four years ago.

Linda dropped in every other day with a laundry list of questions regarding Jeremy's past. She came more for confirmation as she worked to piece everything together for the trial. The questions became fewer as they approached the start date, and he figured that was a good sign, that Linda had filled the supposed gaps in his story.

"I think we're in as good a position as we can be," she said three days before the trial. It was Friday afternoon and she had just one final weekend to prepare for opening statements.

"Is there anything you don't feel ready for?" Jeremy asked.

"No. My interviews have been good. Clark and Dr. Siva had a lot of great things to say about you. I like to think we have enough to convince the jury against death. At the end of the day, that's the goal, anything extra is a bonus."

Easy for you to say when it's not your life on the line.

"Is there anything else I need to do for the trial?"

"No. Like I've said, just keep quiet, don't engage. Be attentive to the witnesses, but never show emotion. Someone in the jury will always have an eye on you."

"Okay, easy enough."

With that, Linda left Jeremy for the weekend. When he returned to his cell, Jeremy did something he hadn't done in more than two years. He laid on his cot facing the ceiling, and joined his hands below his chin.

"Dear God, please forgive me for my sins. Please protect me from death and allow me to continue my work to make the world a better place. Too many of your children live in darkness every day. Amen."

Tears ran from his eyes into his ears. His mind had felt chaotic for the last two weeks, with all the preparation and seeing his parents. Praying helped put his mind at ease and he wished he had been doing it since day one.

The rest of the weekend dragged worse than normal. Time took forever to pass when all you could do was look at the ceiling and try to puzzle your life together.

On Sunday, Jeremy saved his pill underneath his tongue when he received it in the morning, stashed it under his pillow when the officer left, and swallowed it after dinner. He felt anxious all morning and knew he'd need the assistance with sleep later on. He had no windows in his cell but could see the daylight shine down in the hallway outside of his door, in golden rays. The beauty of nature could apparently find its way into the ugliest of places.

His mind drifted as he lay on his bed all afternoon. He pondered the trial, envisioning all of the jurors now responsible for the outcome of his life. He fell in and out of sleep, before finally dozing into a deep sleep in the evening and through the night.

20

Chapter 20

Sunday, October 22, 2017

Cathleen Speidel had tried to keep busy in the weeks leading up to the trial before her days would consist of sitting in a courtroom and hearing violent, disturbing testimony.

The trial had placed a damper on her upcoming travel plans for the fall. A trip to Las Vegas had been arranged, just like every autumn for the last several years, but now the trip was postponed until the conclusion of the trial. As a former airline employee, her flight was easily rescheduled, but delaying her relaxing week at the casino made her miserable.

She knew she'd be selected to the jury as soon as she arrived the courthouse back in August. She'd served as a juror twice before, and that experience always made her an automatic favorite. The questionnaire she filled out upon arriving made her suspect she would be a prime target. While they didn't ask directly, the questions strongly suggested they wanted jurors who had free time to spare, in anticipation of a lengthy trial. They also preferred candidates with minimal TV, technology, and social media exposure.

As a 65-year-old single woman, she checked all of these

boxes. As suspected, she was asked into the courtroom, where the attorneys would question her further. She froze when she entered and saw the man who had killed all those people, sitting calmly beside his defense team dressed in a dark red jumpsuit.

This is for his *trial?*

All the worries about her trip vanished. She *wanted* this trial. It would be historic, and who wouldn't want to be a part of history? Vegas wasn't going anywhere. She immediately told the attorneys she had a wide open schedule and would have no issues committing to a longer trial. They projected three to four weeks, which really wasn't that long. During her time in the courtroom, she looked out the corner of her eye toward Jeremy Heston. And while her glasses didn't allow her a clear view from that angle, she could sense him staring back at her.

The attorneys grilled her with questions about her family's history, digging for any sort of connection to mental illness. There were none, and after a couple hours Cathleen was informed that they would follow up should they choose her as a juror. This process was different than the common procedure where jurors were informed the same day, but she recalled seeing the number of jury summons had been record-breaking for this case.

As she thought back on all of these events, she felt a tingle of excitement knowing the trial would begin tomorrow. On this particular night, Cathleen had just returned from a trip to the grocery store. She liked to go at night time when there was less of a crowd and no lines.

A cool breeze blew her short, sandy brown hair in crazy waves when she stepped out of her car at home. A full moon lit up her block and she could hear a distant squeal of teenagers playing a game of hide-and-seek. Leaves rustled across her lawn as

97

she stood behind her open trunk, examining which bags of groceries to take inside, and which to leave in her freezer in the garage. Boxes of frozen dinners had spilled out of their bags and all around the trunk.

Cathleen sighed as she collected the boxes; she didn't hear the soft footsteps approaching from behind. The shuffling steps silenced directly behind her, and the dark figure watched as she gathered the groceries.

Cathleen felt eyes on her, but it wasn't uncommon for a neighbor to be on a late-night stroll around the block.

When she turned, her heart leapt through her throat as she saw the hooded figure. The darkness provided camouflage too, along with the black clothing and the baggy hood over the head.

"Cathleen," a steady man's voice said from the pit of darkness where his face would be.

Cathleen's throat locked and she couldn't speak. Quickly, the man's hand grasped her and clenched tightly around her neck. She sucked in air with short, panicked gasps. The man's fingers felt soft, and she assumed he was wearing gloves. The glow from the garage light revealed the whites of the man's eyes, staring at her as his grip loosened just enough for her to breathe normally.

"Ms. Speidel," the man said, this time in a formal and articulate voice. "I know you're on the Jeremy Heston jury. I need you to make sure he receives the verdict of not guilty by reason of insanity."

He paused as if awaiting a response, but he still had her throat grasped, so as to not allow speech.

"Anything less will be very bad for you."

A gust of wind howled and whistled, prompting the man to look behind him. She could feel his hand trembling beneath the glove and wondered if he was nervous.

"If he receives any sort of guilty verdict, I'll be back. I know where your son lives and I'll slit his throat faster than you can say 'not guilty.' All you have to do is become the jury foreman, and make sure to influence your peers to see things your way."

Tears rolled down Cathleen's face and adrenaline flowed through her veins. The lack of oxygen to her head made her eyeballs feel like they would explode out of their sockets.

"My instructions are simple: get him the insanity verdict, and I'll leave you $100,000 cash as a thank you. I understand the risk you're taking, so I want to make sure you're taken care of. If he gets a guilty verdict, I'll be paying a visit to Ironwood Street in San Diego."

David. That was where Cathleen's adult son lived. Whoever the hooded figure was, he was not bluffing.

The man released his grip and watched as she huffed and puffed for fresh air. He took a step back before speaking again.

"Make it happen, Cathleen. And if you speak of this confrontation to anyone, I *will* find out, and I'll come back here. If I have to come back here for any other reason besides delivering the $100,000, it won't be a pretty sight for you."

The man pivoted around and broke into a sprint. His rapid footsteps faded away into silence within seconds.

Cathleen rubbed her throat, where the throbbing pain remained from the man's fingers. Every inhale felt like sharp needles in her throat. She looked in the direction the man had run and saw nothing but darkness, street lights glowing softly over the deserted street.

What do I do? Call the cops right now?

She wanted nothing more than to do just that, but she resisted.

How could this man know if I contact the authorities?

Perhaps he knew someone within the court system, or even worked in the system himself. That would explain how he knew she was a juror in the case.

But why would he want to fix the trial to end this way?

He was surely a friend or relative of Jeremy's. Who else would go to such an extreme measure?

Cathleen returned to taking her groceries inside as her mind raced. She looked over her shoulder every time she returned to her car, but she knew he was long gone and not coming back any time soon.

He could be bluffing.

If the man was bluffing, she could call the police and notify the judge without a worry. But what would she tell them? She didn't even get a clear look at the man and had no way to describe him except for his approximate height and the tone of his voice.

And if he's not bluffing?

The thought sent chills throughout her body, and she shivered underneath her sweater. If he meant everything he said, then she had no choice but to try and influence the verdict. She didn't need his money, but she didn't want to die from something out of her control. Or worse, have something happen to David.

I could run away.

Cathleen entertained the thought. She could finally get the condo she wanted in Las Vegas, or live on an island somewhere and drink fruity cocktails all day. With more years behind her than ahead, the idea wasn't too shabby. Living the island life for the next ten to fifteen years could be relaxing. All she'd need to pack would be books and clothes. She could leave Denver behind forever and be a fugitive of the United States for fleeing from a trial.

Don't be silly. You live here. Your life is here.

She'd *wanted* to work on this jury, looked forward to it, but now it was all tainted by the hooded man.

Cathleen poured a glass of wine to the brim, knowing sleep would be hopeless without a little help. She could still feel her body pulsing in anxiety at the violent encounter.

Once the wine kicked in, she felt she had the courage to do the right thing and took out her cell phone, punching in 9-1-1 on the number pad. She stared at the three numbers in her trembling hand, her thumb hovering over the green button to place the call.

He has David's address.

Cathleen canceled the call and ran to the bathroom to vomit. She was about to be sucked into a conspiracy much worse than fleeing the country, and there was nothing she could do about it.

21

Chapter 21

Monday, October 23, 2017
  Day 1 of the trial

Jeremy declined breakfast, his body trembling from a monsoon of nerves. Looking at him, someone might have thought he had Parkinson's; he'd never felt so many nerves working their way through his body. Like creatures crawling beneath his flesh in search of a way out.

It's time. This is really happening.

He wasn't conscious of the drive to the courthouse, his mind racing out of control as the outdoors passed by the window. As of today, his life was officially in the hands of a jury of nine women and three men who had never met him.

A dozen news vans filled the court's parking lot as they pulled around to the back entrance. Police had blocked the area to protect Jeremy from reporters and photographers. His escort led him to his private holding room in which to change into his suit. Gray slacks and a navy jacket waited on the table with a white button-up to wear underneath.

Jeremy changed quickly and made his way to the courtroom.

It was his first public appearance where he didn't look like a criminal, and the crowd fell silent as he entered and started toward Linda. He had gone through this exact motion several times already, but today felt like the start of a new game. The cameras were on now, and the whole world could watch if they wanted. Every single move from here on out would be greatly scrutinized. Geoff glared at Jeremy when he sat down, and Linda returned the glare at the prosecution table.

"All rise!"

Judge Zamora entered the courtroom, settled behind his bench. He sat down and began speaking. "Good morning, ladies and gentlemen. I look forward to finally beginning this trial. It's been a long road and I hope you're all prepared. Does counsel have any matters to discuss before we bring in the jury?"

"No, Your Honor," Geoff and Linda said in unison.

"Let's bring in the jury."

The bailiff opened the door next to the jury box and all eyes turned to the twenty-four people walking in. Some jurors grinned nervously while others kept their eyes to the floor en route to their seat.

Jeremy noticed the older woman who had stared at him before sat in the first seat in the front row now. She still had a stern expression and peered at Jeremy from behind her glasses, causing the hairs on his arms to prickle.

"Good morning, jurors," Judge Zamora said. "I want to cover a few things before we get started today.

"First, please remember that a camera is live in the courtroom and broadcasting the trial worldwide. Be assured that your identity is protected, as none of you will appear on camera at any point in this trial. Should you choose to speak with the press at the conclusion of the trial, that is at your discretion.

"At no point are you to discuss the trial with friends, family, the press, members of counsel, nor among yourselves—until after all evidence has been presented and the defense rests their case. Until then feel free to talk with each other about anything else in the world.

"Last, and most important, remember this case is based on mental illness. The defendant has pleaded not guilty by reason of insanity and therefore the burden has been placed on the prosecution to prove beyond a reasonable doubt that the defendant was sane during the time of the crimes.

"I will remind you of this again when the time comes, but please keep it in consideration throughout the whole trial. Now we're about to begin with opening statements. Opening statements are not meant to be used as evidence, but rather as an outline for what you can expect to be covered during the course of the trial. Any questions from the jury before we begin?"

The jurors looked around at each other and shook their heads.

"Okay, Mr. Batchelor, you may begin with your opening statement."

Geoff rose from his table. He wore a navy jacket and pants with subtle gray pinstripes, a light blue undershirt, and a blue and gray checkered tie with a double Windsor knot. He looked every bit the district attorney, with his blond hair styled to perfection.

He held a small remote in his hand and pointed it to the TV screen on the wall opposite the jury, directly to Jeremy's left. The TV flickered to life and revealed a familiar picture.

A beige door with a stainless steel handle, surrounded by white walls and a black keypad to the right. It was the side entrance into the Open Hands office. Jeremy's stomach jumped at the sight and he felt the weight of the world once again wearing down on him.

Geoff shuffled across the room and positioned himself in front of the jury. They looked at the TV and back to him as he stared at the ground, collecting his thoughts. It seemed like an eternity to Jeremy before he started speaking.

"Behind this door is horror," Geoff said, pointing to the image behind him. "Behind this door are bullets...brains...blood...and bodies. Behind this door, one man who thought he had lost his career, lost his love life, lost his purpose, came to execute a massacre."

Geoff paused, pointed the remote to the screen, and everyone watched as the image of the door gave way to an all black screen. Sound started to pour out of the TV's speakers.

"911, please state your emergency," a voice said.

"Please send help," a shaky female voice cried. "We're at the Open Hands office and there's a shooter. There's bodies everywhere. Please help."

The sound of bullets firing filled the dead air, along with piercing screams, before the sound clip abruptly ended.

Geoff strode toward Jeremy until he stood five feet in front him, still facing the jury. He raised a finger and pointed it directly at Jeremy—into his soul, it felt—without looking at him.

"This man murdered thirteen people on March 11, 2016. Thirteen innocent people. Thirteen people who had woken up that morning to go to work like any other day. Thirteen people who were excited that it was Friday and had a fun weekend ahead. Thirteen people who never went home after kissing their families good-bye in the morning. This guy did that."

Geoff's bony finger seemed to dig into Jeremy before he lowered his hand and returned to the jury.

"You're going to hear a lot in this trial about mental health and mental illness. While that may very well be a factor, I ask that you keep an open mind to the bigger narrative taking place.

"The months leading up to March 11 were filled with disappointment and rejection for Jeremy Heston. He had worked with his company for nearly four years, gaining respect over that time, and was positioned for a long and successful career with the company. When opportunity presented itself in the form a promotion, he applied for it. Who wouldn't? We've all reached that point when it's time to reach for more.

"But he was rejected for this promotion, and it crippled his spirits. Shortly after, another opportunity became available, one you could argue he'd been groomed to do. Now, I want you to pay close attention to this specific time frame.

"He's once again rejected for the promotion, and at the same time, he has to deal with the ending of a long romantic relationship. With two rejected promotions and a breakup—all within a six-week window—his work performance clearly declines, as you'll see. It declines so badly that he's placed on disciplinary action.

"This disciplinary action took place in early January, two months prior to him opening fire on his coworkers. The month following this, he made clear progress with his work performance, and for a brief moment it seemed everything had returned to normal—until late February, when the company started its annual review process.

"Now, Jeremy did *not* receive a pay raise, after having received a raise of at least ten percent every year the prior three years. Two weeks after that, paperwork had been written up to terminate his employment with the company after four years of service. The date for his termination? March 11, 2016. The very day he walked into his office with an AR-15 assault rifle and massacred his coworkers.

"Now, let's look at the big picture here. Two promotion rejections, one breakup, one stiffed raise, and one pending job termination. With the exception of the breakup, all these events had one common denominator: Shelly Williams."

Geoff clicked the remote and a portrait of Shelly, her husband, and her daughter posing in front of a lake filled the screen.

"Shelly Williams was the director of the customer service department for Open Hands and was involved in every decision regarding this guy's future with the company. More important, Shelly was a mother to a 13-year-old girl who just started high school last month. This young woman no longer has a mother to guide her through the most difficult years of her life.

"You will see later that Shelly was the first person shot in this vicious attack. Coincidence? I think not. I propose that this crime was an act of revenge. I propose he had every intent to kill Shelly Williams that day, before panic spread across the office and he reacted by firing his weapon at anything moving."

Geoff clicked his remote again. A portrait of Mark now filled the screen, grinning and full of life.

"This is Mark Fernandez. Mark was hired as Jeremy's manager after he was rejected for the same position. Mark was the second person shot after Shelly Williams had collapsed at her desk. Mark was also involved in the rejected raise and the pending termination. That means the first two people shot were the two people who had made this guy's life a living hell."

Geoff clicked, and Jeremy's heart sunk. A picture of a smiling Sylvia filled the screen, along with her son, who had the same smile as his mother.

"Sylvia Hamilton. Sylvia worked directly with the shooter and was a good friend to him. Why she deserved to go as part of his sick game is beyond me. She was mother to the 9-year-old boy you see in this picture—another child who now has to live the rest of his life without a mother."

Click.

"This is Janae Valdez. Janae had moved to Denver from Texas in hopes of starting a long career with Open Hands. She was even interviewed by the shooter as part of her initial screening. She was only 23 years old."

Oh, Janae, I should've never hired you.

Click.

"This is Cherie Robinson. Cherie was Janae's best friend. She was found dead in the office right at Janae's side. Both Cherie and Janae worked on the same team as the shooter. Cherie was 27 and left behind a 5-year-old girl and a 3-year-old boy."

Sorry, Cherie, I never had anything against you.

Click.

"This is Terri Sharpe. Terri had been with the company for six years and was involved with the interviewing and hiring of the shooter. She worked as a manager in the department and was well loved. Terri was 32 and leaves behind a husband of three years."

Jeremy thought back to his first interview at E-Nonymous when Terri and Trevor welcomed him so graciously to the company.

Click.

"This is Charlie Chappell. Charlie worked in the customer service department. This was his first job out of college. He was a soft-spoken person who liked to connect with his teammates and always brought a smile to others. Charlie was 22 years old."

Jeremy had chatted with Charlie a few times, but never really knew him.

Click.

"This is Ian Hagy. Ian was hired on shortly after Jeremy, but had never worked directly with him. Ian was shot while trying to save others. He was banging a chair against the barricaded door that Jeremy used to keep everyone trapped in the office while he took his time. Ian was 31 years old."

You were a good guy, Ian.

Click.

"This is Erin Hoffman. Erin started with the company only two months prior to the shooting. She was the mother of two adult children and was looking forward to working what she considered to be her final job before retiring to sail the world with her husband. She was 52"

I have no idea who you are, Erin.

Click.

"This is Tanya Vegas. Tanya had recently become a U.S. citizen after her four years of college at the University of Michigan. This was her first job after college too. She was 21 years old and leaves behind six younger siblings in Argentina."

Jeremy remembered briefly meeting Tanya and admired her beauty. He had tried talking to her a few months after Jamie dumped him, but nothing ever came of it.

Click.

"This is Kevin Woodland. Kevin worked as a salesman for the company. One of the sales teams had a meeting that day on the customer service level and he was one of the three who lost their lives in that meeting. He died covering and saving his girlfriend, who also worked with the company. He was 26 years old."

Another good guy.

Click.

"This is Daniel Rodriguez. Daniel was one of the highest-performing salesmen in the company's history. He was leading the training class that day, teaching new salesmen how to become the best at their roles. He was a leader on the sales floor and would get to know everyone that joined the company on a personal level. He was 32."

The top salesman in the Denver office, everybody loved you.

Click.

"Last but not least, this is B.J. Reynolds. B.J. was killed trying to crawl out of the training room after the shooter had entered. He was also part of a newly hired group of salespeople. B.J. was 25 years old."

Geoff paused to return to his table and have a sip of water.

"I want you to remember these thirteen faces. These people did nothing to deserve the fate they received on March 11. They had all gone into work, to make their company and their world a better place, before this guy decided to act on his selfish, violent impulses and unleash hell on everyone who got in his way."

Geoff returned to his seat and wrote in his notebook. Linda, who had been taking notes throughout the opening statement, continued doing so as Wilbert rose from his seat and approached the jury. Jeremy had never noticed how tall Wilbert stood; he towered over the jury box. He'd never spoken directly with him either. Linda had always been the one to come to the jail, and Jeremy wondered why Wilbert was now the one giving their opening statement. Despite his older age, he appeared refreshed, standing in front of the jury in a suit as fine as Geoff's, with a perfectly groomed beard. He put on a pair of glasses as he cleared his throat.

"Ladies and gentlemen of the jury, Mr. Batchelor just provided us with a rather engaging story. Like Judge Zamora said earlier, this is a trial of mental illness. I'm not going to stand here and try to convince you that my client didn't commit these heinous crimes. He did. He killed thirteen people and wounded twenty-two others—that is a fact. I will, however, convince you that there are many holes in Mr. Batchelor's story, with regard to what this case is actually about. You'll be left to decide whether my client was sane or insane during the attack on his office.

"While the narrative provided by Mr. Batchelor may make sense on the surface, I ask you to take a closer look at the details. There's a reason why he asked you to look at the big picture, and that's because if you look at the facts up close, his story simply does not add up.

"You'll hear from one of the top psychiatrists in the world. She'll paint a clear picture of a dormant mental illness that became disturbed and elevated to a breaking point. Sure, the events mentioned by Mr. Batchelor, at my client's workplace in the months prior, contributed to his actions, but you'll see how it was really his mental illness that blurred the lines of reality within Mr. Heston's mind.

"The murders committed were disgusting and vile. But by the time Mr. Heston stepped into the office, his perception of reality was so skewed, he no longer lived in the same world we live in. To him, this world seemed as real as this seems to you right now.

"Mental illness runs in Mr. Heston's family, and his ancestor had suffered from disturbing episodes as a result. The defendant has suffered through a serious, undiagnosed disorder. The disorder poisoned his mind the same way cancer poisons the body.

"Throughout this case you'll be hearing a lot about Mr. Batchelor's story and also about mental health. Mental health is backed by science. We can't ever ignore cold, hard science.

"For someone sane to pull off a violent outburst like this would require some sort of planning. The evidence presented in this trial will show you that no matter how defeated Mr. Heston may have felt by the happenings in his life, at no point is there proof to show that this attack was planned. Mr. Heston went to bed on March 10 with a disease plaguing his mind, and when he woke up on the 11th he decided to act on that disease by grabbing the rifle he had owned for quite some time and taking it to his office.

"As for Shelly Williams and Mark Fernandez being the first two people shot, that can simply be explained by their location relative to Mr. Heston's entrance. Shelly sat no more than ten feet in front of him when he entered the room, and Mark was the next closest to her. Don't let some romanticized story of revenge trick you into believing something that's simply not there.

"Mr. Heston had improved his working relationship with Shelly and Mark—you'll find that documented just as much as his discipline was documented a month prior. His closest friend in the office is on the list of victims you just saw. No sane person is going to shoot their friend, especially with no reason to do so.

"You're all sane people. You can all probably relate to the struggles that Mr. Heston had gone through. You've likely found yourself in the same position as him: turned down for a job, turned down for a raise, turned down from a relationship with someone you loved. Sane people can handle these issues through other means. Sane people would look for a new job elsewhere after so much rejection. Sane people know when to let go of a relationship and wait for someone new. Sane people don't take a gun to their office and shoot everyone in sight. That's what an *insane* person does.

"Put yourself in his position and imagine how you'd handle each problem that arose. How could you do that if you'd lost all sense of reality? Psychiatry easily explains how these external factors built up to Mr. Heston's snapping point.

"You'll notice over the course of this trial that Mr. Heston may seem distracted, aloof, or disconnected at times, and that is because of the medication he has been prescribed. Please do the right thing and make sure Mr. Heston receives the care he needs: in a mental institution, not in jail. Thank you."

Wilbert returned to his seat next to Linda. Geoff glared at him as he passed. The jury relaxed after sitting rigid for both opening statements, some of their faces pale.

Judge Zamora broke the silence. "Thank you, counsel. Jurors, please remember that opening statements are not to be used as evidence. Everything that was just discussed will be further fleshed out over the trial, with actual testimony and evidence. I want to take a quick fifteen-minute recess before we begin with the first witness. We'll meet back here at 11 a.m. sharp."

Judge Zamora banged his gavel, and chatter immediately erupted in the courtroom.

Here we go, Jeremy thought. *Let's see what these lawyers can do.*

22

Chapter 22

Monday, October 23, 2017

Ricky Heston sat toward the back of the courtroom, palms sweating, his suit jacket absorbing moisture from his armpits. Seeing Jeremy's victims flash by on the screen made the whole thing seem real again after eighteen months.

He listened to the opening statements while staring at the back of Jeremy's head, wondering how his nephew had taken such a nasty turn in life. He remembered taking him to so many sporting events as a kid, and seeing Jeremy's face light up every time they walked up the steps at different stadiums. His nephew had been so happy all the time, full of life, and he ached at the thought of what he had done to all those innocent lives.

Ricky had been informed by the district attorney that he would be the first witness called to the stand.

"I want to set Jeremy's background with guns right off the bat," the D.A. had told him over the phone.

It felt like he was working against his nephew, but had no choice. *Just answer the questions. And keep those spent shells out of your mind!*

Ricky had flown in a week earlier to settle back into town and prepare for his testimony. The high altitude had caused his skin to shrivel up like a raisin after living at sea level for over a year. Despite his itchy flesh, Ricky loved being back in his home city.

He caught up with his brother and sister-in-law, and they filled him in on every detail of the trial—it seemed they might have known more than the lawyers after obsessing over every bit of released information. Despite their morbid fascination with the trial, he thought they seemed almost back to their normal selves, considering the circumstances. Robert thanked him for coming back home to contribute to the trial, even though he was the prosecution's witness.

The week flew by and Ricky was thankful. Being stuck in the middle of the trial made him want to get away, and he'd planned to catch the first flight back to Florida tomorrow.

He hadn't dared visit his cabin, wanting to keep it as far out of his mind as possible. The lawyers had never asked about the cabin in the pretrial questionnaires, so he assumed there would be no surprises on the witness stand. Besides, they never presented a warrant of any sort to search his property, meaning they didn't know about the cabin.

Ricky had no real reason to be nervous for his testimony, but he was. He watched as the judge entered the courtroom again, knowing his number would be called within minutes.

They don't know about the cabin. The shell is sunk in the middle of the Atlantic Ocean.

"Mr. Batchelor, your first witness, please," Judge Zamora said once the jury had settled into their seats. Silence and tension filled the air as everyone awaited the trial's first witness. Who would it be? What would they say?

The D.A. stood, buttoned his jacket, and said, "The prosecution calls Richard Heston to the stand."

Ricky stood and felt all eyes in the audience immediately turn to him. The gallery was only eight rows, with an aisle separating the two sides. Jeremy was on Ricky's left as he approached the bar and pushed open the swinging door. Robert sat in the front row behind Jeremy and nodded to Ricky when their eyes locked. He could see the pain and anxiety in his brother's brown eyes.

Jeremy had sat up stiffly, Ricky noticed, when his uncle's name was called. *He must not have known I was being called as a witness,* Ricky thought.

He walked to the witness stand at the judge's right, and the bailiff approached him.

"Please raise your right hand," the bailiff said. "Do you swear to tell the truth, the whole truth, and nothing but the truth?"

"I do," Ricky said and sat down in his chair, adjusting the microphone to his level.

"Please state your full name for the record," Geoff said from the podium.

"Richard Jeremy Heston."

"Thank you, Mr. Heston. Can you please tell us how you're related to the defendant?"

"I'm his uncle. He's my brother's son."

Good, Ricky thought. *Stay cool.*

"Would you say you've been involved in the defendant's life?"

"Yes, for the most part."

"What sort of activities would you and your nephew partake in?"

"Mostly sporting events. We've been to a lot of Nuggets games, Broncos games, and like to golf as well."

"Would one of those sports be recreational shooting?"

God damn it.

"Yes, sir."

"How often did you go shooting with your nephew?"

"We've been to the shooting range a couple times together and hunting at least once a year for quite a while."

"When was the last time you were at a shooting range with your nephew?"

"It was toward the end of 2012, a little before Christmas."

"And your last hunting trip with him?"

"Would've been the same year, in November."

"Would you say your nephew was a good shot?"

"Objection, Your Honor!" Linda jumped out of her seat, startling Jeremy, who had become entranced at the sight of the uncle he hadn't seen in years. "Speculation."

"Sustained," the judge barked.

Geoff returned to questioning. "Mr. Heston, can you tell us about your background with firearms?"

"I served in the Marines for ten years as a Gunner. I was responsible for conducting arms-based training."

"So it's safe to say you're experienced with firearms?"

"Very much so."

"Do you still have any firearms from your days with the Marines?"

Fuck.

"Yes, sir."

"What kind?"

"I still have my M-16 and a couple of pistols."

"Did you ever take your M-16 rifle to the shooting range with your nephew?"

"Yes, sir."

"Did your nephew ever shoot your M-16?"

Ricky paused, not wanting to answer the question.

"Mr. Heston?"

"Yes, he has."

"How many times did your nephew use your M-16?"

"Just once, at our last trip to the range."

"At the range, you are shooting at a target. How many shots did your nephew successfully hit the target?"

"About half."

"Not bad for his first time."

Ricky shrugged his shoulders.

"Would you consider an AR-15 to be similar to an M-16?"

Ricky paused and put on his best thinking face. "They're similar in build, but in terms of performance are fairly different."

"Can you elaborate on those differences?"

"Yes. An M-16 is a fully automatic weapon. You can hold the trigger down and it keeps firing rounds until you let go. It's also much more powerful than an AR-15. An AR-15 is a semiautomatic weapon, meaning you have to pull the trigger for each shot you want to take. In short, an M-16 is designed to kill people, and an AR-15 is a recreational firearm."

Way to tiptoe around that question.

"Do you know the state of Colorado's law for the maximum amount of rounds that can be loaded into a firearm?"

"Yes, sir. Ten."

"Evidence shows that your nephew had not just one, but five magazines, each designed to hold not ten but *thirty* rounds. These are not sold in this state. Do you know how to obtain one of these magazines?"

"It's like anything else—you can find them online or for sale on the black market."

"How much time would it take for you to empty a magazine of thirty rounds with an AR-15?"

Ricky pursed his lips before answering. "Probably just under thirty seconds."

"No further questions." Geoff returned to his seat as Linda approached the podium.

"Good morning, Mr. Heston. I have just a few questions for you."

Ricky nodded nervously.

"Did your nephew ever express an interest in rifles after he used your M-16?"

"Not to me."

"When was the last time you saw your nephew in person?"

"I actually haven't seen him since that last trip to the shooting range in 2012."

"So a little under five years?"

"Correct."

"It sounds like you and he were pretty close. Why the five-year hiatus?"

"I travel a lot for work. I'm usually gone at least two weeks each month. Once he graduated college and joined the real world he made his own friends and started living his life."

"You didn't even see him over the holidays?"

"I'm always on the road for major holidays, so no."

"You ever speak to him on the phone?"

"A couple times, but mostly by text message, to talk about things happening in the sports world."

"According to our records, your nephew never visited another shooting range since your last time with him. Did he ever mention anything about going back?"

"No."

"In your professional opinion, is an AR-15 the sort of weapon that can simply be picked up and learned on the spot?"

"No."

"Would it require a lot of practice to master?"

"Yes. The rule of thumb is that you need to fire at least a thousand rounds before you can fully learn your firearm."

"And how many rounds did your nephew fire the day he used your M-16?"

"Only one magazine, so ten rounds."

"No further questions. Thank you."

Ricky didn't know how long he hadn't been breathing, but he let out a long exhale when Linda returned to her seat.

I'm home free.

"Mr. Heston, you are excused. Thank you for your testimony," Judge Zamora said.

"Thank you," he replied, before standing up to exit the witness box. Jeremy stared at him, trying to force eye contact, but Ricky's eyes locked with Jeremy's lips instead; he couldn't bring himself to look his monster of a nephew in the eyes. Jeremy was the reason he could no longer go to his cabin, the reason for him moving all the way across the country this past year.

Jeremy, you stupid motherfucker.

Ricky walked out of the courtroom and decided to head to the airport right away.

23

Chapter 23

Wednesday, October 25, 2017
  Day 3 of the trial

The first two days of the trial were filled with much repetitive testimony. Dozens of Open Hands sales reps were called to the stand, telling their story from the floor above the shooting. They each spoke of a sound like fireworks exploding beneath their feet. No, they didn't hear any screams, just the repetitive firing of Jeremy's rifle.

Someone from the H.R. department had barged onto the sales floor, screaming, "There's a shooter downstairs! Get under a desk or lock yourself in a conference room!"

A couple sales reps had been on their way down the stairs when the attack started. "Run!" someone shouted, prompting the sales reps to turn around and get the fuck out. A group of fortunate survivors had gathered in the parking lot as the S.W.A.T. team arrived in two black armored trucks.

You've done something special when the S.W.A.T. team arrives, Jeremy thought. He had never considered how his shooting might have sounded on the sales floor above, but had a clear picture now that he heard from nearly every sales rep in the building that day. A few faces looked familiar, but most were coworkers he'd never actually met.

The S.W.A.T. members and other first responders also testified for the prosecution. They spoke of a "horror movie" scene when they entered the office to the sight of blood, intestines, and dead bodies everywhere.

One of the first police officers to arrive on site, Jordan Shepard, gave a heartbreaking testimony about saving Elayna Avery's life.

"I walked in, saw at least two dozen bodies on the ground. It was impossible to know whether they were dead, wounded, or playing dead. In the far corner I saw the young man we believed to be the shooter. We already had him in cuffs by the time I entered. But on the other side of the office I saw a young blond woman on the ground shivering, and I ran to her.

"She had blood pouring from the top of her head and her eyes kept rolling back and forth while her lips tried to speak. I knew she probably had only a matter of minutes to live, so I picked her up, ran out of the building, and laid her in the backseat of my squad car."

Officer Shepard paused, tears streaming down his face.

"I've never driven so fast in my life. I was going 150 down Arapahoe Road toward the hospital with my sirens blaring, and I could still hear her in the back seat gasping for air.

"'Don't die on me!' I yelled. 'Don't fucking die on me!'

"I saved her life. I checked in with her every single day while she was in the hospital—for six months—recovering from the gunshot to her head."

Officer Shepard broke into sobs.

"Thank you for your testimony, Officer Shepard," Geoff said.

"I know that was extremely difficult to relive."

Linda declined to cross-examine the witness, leaving the heavy emotions to fill the courtroom. Jeremy was glad to hear Elayna had survived, and wondered if she'd make an appearance as a witness.

* * *

Once the emotional stories were finished, Jeremy looked forward to the testimony from his old friend and manager, Nicole. Her testimony wasn't nearly as big a deal to the lawyers compared to other witnesses, but Jeremy wanted to know what she had to say.

She had always defended Jeremy, and knew the bullshit he had to climb through to try and impress Shelly. She also worked closely with Shelly and knew what really happened behind the scenes. What Jeremy really wanted to know was the truth as to why Shelly had made his career a living hell.

Now, he would hopefully find out.

"The prosecution calls Nicole Fisk," Geoff Batchelor said.

Jeremy wanted desperately to turn in his chair, to look Nicole in the eyes as she walked to the witness box, but that would show his hand, considering he hadn't done it for anyone else.

Instead he kept his stare fixed on the witness box and watched as Nicole's skinny body passed through his vision, her golden hair flowing behind her, until she stood in the box with a thin arm elevated to swear in. He didn't remember her being so skinny.

"Good morning, Ms. Fisk," Geoff started. "Can you please

tell us how you know the defendant?"

"Good morning. Yes. I worked with him during his entire time at Open Hands. We started as peers until I was eventually promoted and he started to work for me after his promotion."

"You were his direct manager?"

"Yes. He also worked closely with me as a sort of confidant once he became a team lead."

"Can you explain the hierarchy of your department for the jury, please?"

"When you start with the customer service department, regardless of which individual team you're on, you begin as a representative. The next level from there is a team lead, where you are given more responsibility. After that is the manager role, which I was and currently still am." Nicole spoke in her usual squeaky voice, but Jeremy could tell she was nervous by the way she fidgeted with her fingers. If he could see her legs, they'd probably be bouncing out of control. She, too, was avoiding eye contact with him.

"Thank you. Were you involved in the decisions regarding the defendant's potential promotions?"

"My opinion was sought out, but I had no say in the final decision."

"And who did?"

"Shelly Williams."

"And where did Mrs. Williams fit into the hierarchy of roles?"

"She was at the director level, above me. I reported to her directly."

"I want to talk about the first promotion the defendant applied for. I believe that was the position of head trainer for your department, is that correct?"

"Yes."

"Will you tell us about that interview process? What all did it entail?"

"Jeremy had a brief and informal first-round interview with Shelly. Every other candidate had to interview in full with Shelly and other managers from our department, but she decided to just give him a casual interview with her since he was already working as our unofficial trainer at the time.

"After that, the second round consisted of a training presentation and panel interview with all the managers of our department."

"What sort of training presentation did the defendant have to prepare?"

"It was open topic. He just had to lead a training for the managers on a topic of his choice."

"And that topic was?"

"How to play poker."

Nicole looked at the ground after this last statement and her face flushed.

"And how did he do?"

"I thought he did very well. It was a fun session and very informative."

"You mentioned the defendant had already been doing the job. Why have him interview and go through this process?"

"I honestly don't know. That wasn't my decision."

"Whose decision was it?"

"Shelly's."

"How long had the defendant been working directly under you at this point in time?"

She scrunched her face in thought. "I believe it was close to two years."

"As he was then reporting to you, did you assist him in his

pursuit of the promotion?"

"I always put in a good word for him. He did terrific work day in and day out. He was a resource for our team and an all around asset to the company."

Nicole, always standing up for me, even after all this, Jeremy thought.

"Were you bothered that he didn't receive the promotion?"

"Yes, I was. I knew how badly he wanted it and how hard he had worked for it. It was hard to see him denied that opportunity."

"In your opinion, should he have received that job?"

"Yes. We took a group vote after his presentation, just us managers, and I absolutely voted yes."

"How long after the interview was the news delivered to the defendant that he would not be receiving the promotion?"

"It was the end of that same week. On Friday."

"And how did he react?"

"He was bothered, like anyone would be. I encouraged him to take an extended lunch break that day."

"How was his work performance after this decision?"

"It suffered for a couple weeks, but Jeremy bounced back. I knew it was a big blow for him after working so hard."

"Did he ever show any signs of violence?"

"No."

"Any signs of hatred toward Shelly?"

"Hatred? No. He definitely wasn't pleased with Shelly, but nothing hateful was ever said."

"What can you tell me about the second job he was denied for?"

"It was for my job. I was offered an opportunity to manage our billing team and accepted, leaving my position vacant."

"Were you involved in hiring your replacement?"

"Only in leaving a recommendation for who should replace me, and I chose Jeremy."

"Did you know Jeremy would be rejected after your referral?"

Nicole hesitated and now locked eyes with Jeremy. He could sense that she wished she had come clean with him from the start.

"Yes. Shelly told me Jeremy wouldn't be considered."

"Did she give you any reasons why?"

"All she said was that he wasn't ready to manage a team."

"Did you tell Jeremy this, or did he find out from Shelly later?"

"I didn't tell him anything."

"Do you have any knowledge of his performance after this rejection?"

"I don't. I was already in my new department by the time the news was delivered."

"Did you still work with Shelly?"

"Not really. I stayed on the same floor, just around the corner from my old team, but I had a new director to report to and only saw Shelly in passing."

"It's my understanding that you were around the corner when the gunshots started. Did you have any idea who was shooting?"

"Objection!" Linda shouted, shaking her head.

"Sustained," Judge Zamora barked.

Geoff paused as he looked down at his notes. "No further questions."

Linda stood, straightening her sky blue suit as she approached the podium. Nicole cleared her throat and sipped a glass of water that was on the witness stand.

"Ms. Fisk, you stated that Mr. Heston's performance dropped after the rejection. Had you ever seen a drop in his performance before?" she asked in a cold tone.

"No," Nicole said, shifting in her chair. "He was always a strong and consistent performer. I never had to have discussions about his productivity."

"Did Shelly Williams give any reasons for going with another candidate for the trainer position?"

"Yes, she told Jeremy that he lacked passion for the position and that the position required more of a leadership mentality, to grow the role into an eventual department of its own."

"Did she tell you any other reasons in private?"

"We didn't have any discussions in private about the decision. I was only informed that we were hiring someone else and asked to be present in the room when the news was delivered to Jeremy."

"I want to ask you about the events after this. A few weeks later, you left your position as the manager for the onboarding team to manage a different team, is that correct?"

"Yes."

"And Mr. Heston expressed a strong desire to fill the role you had vacated?"

"Yes."

"Did you feel he was also qualified for this position of manager?"

"Yes. I'd say even more so than the trainer position. Our team lead program was designed to help strong contributors progress through the organization. Management was the next natural step from there, and I believe Jeremy was ready to take the reins."

"According to documents from your company, Mr. Heston

was denied a chance to even interview for this promotion. Now why on Earth was someone who had been groomed for this very role denied a chance to interview?"

"The decision was made to only allow candidates with prior management experience. Since Jeremy lacked managerial experience, he was denied."

"Who made that decision?"

"I don't know, but it would have come from Shelly or recruiting."

"I'm thinking Shelly. It's becoming clear she had something against Mr. Heston, and went out of her way to make sure he was not given any opportunities. I want to change gears and ask about the day of March 11. Can you tell me how you were able to escape?"

"With my new team, I sat around the corner from where the shooting took place. When I heard gunshots, I looked to my left and saw blood, and saw one of my peers running and then falling after being hit. I ran from my desk in the opposite direction, as did the rest of my team. We all made it outside the building and kept running until we were in the middle of the street."

Nicole started to tear up and wiped away the welled-up fluid with her fingers.

"No further questions."

24

Chapter 24

Friday, October 27, 2017

The first week of the trial was over and Jeremy laid on his cot shivering. That blond D.A. fuck had done a good job of winning over the jury; there was no denying it. His play seemed simple: bombard the jury with repetitive testimony of the massacre's events, to make them feel as if they were there. First responders and wounded survivors telling their accounts of March 11. Every story was the same, with minor personal details altered by each witness.

Linda and Wilbert cross-examined as best they could, but were hindered by emotional testimony and avoided probing the witnesses any further.

Jeremy's body spasmed violently and his teeth chattered as he reflected on the long week behind him. Jeremy felt cold, hard fear pulsing through his veins. Only a week into the trial and it was already clear that he had no chance of surviving a death penalty verdict.

Why on Earth would these people let me walk on the insanity plea? I killed thirteen innocent people and ruined countless lives.

The thought overwhelmed him and he vomited in his toilet, spitting out chunks of the sandwich he'd had earlier in the day. His hands shook out of control as he attempted to wipe the vomit remnants stuck to his lips.

"I'm going to die in prison," he cried on his cot. He thought of how pets were put down with a quick injection that gradually slowed their heartbeat. He would die with regret in his heart after his experiment had gone terribly wrong.

I was in way over my head.

Jeremy spent the rest of the night wondering what death felt like. Was it simply like falling asleep and never waking up? Was there a light? Would his deceased family be waiting for him on the other side?

He wanted nothing more than to fall asleep, but his mind wouldn't allow it. His conscience needed to confront and accept death right now. Every time he closed his eyes the screams from that day echoed. He couldn't recall what the gun sounded like in the quiet office, but the shrills from his coworkers would forever ring loudly in his soul. He remembered how the smell of gun powder and blood had filled the air. He'd never known blood had a smell, but when gallons of the bodily fluid had poured from his victims, the metallic odor hung around.

The images from that day ran through his mind. He'd never taken the time to absorb the scene, always too worried about the next steps he had to take. Blood and bodies scattered across the floor had been all he could remember. Hearing testimony and seeing the crime scene photos had disturbed him in court. The bodies laid out on the ground like stuffed mannequins.

Blackness filled the quiet jail cell; it had to be after midnight. All Jeremy could hear was the ringing sound of silence, his breathing, and those damned screams from over a year ago.

"I should've never done it," he admitted to himself. "I can't die this way, for the whole world to see."

After three more hours had passed, Jeremy pulled the sheet from his cot, tied it around his neck, and pulled the ends tight in opposite directions. It reminded him of the last time he'd worn a tie around his neck, standing outside the Open Hands office as a young and excited college graduate ready to give it to the world.

He squeezed tighter, until the feeling gave way to choking, cutting off the blood supply and oxygen to his head. His fingers lost their strength and released the sheet before he collapsed into darkness.

* * *

Jeremy jolted awake, unsure of how long he'd been out. It could've been five minutes or a couple hours for all he knew, in the darkness. The sheet was still around his neck and he pulled it off quickly, grateful no one had seen. Had an officer walked by and noticed his noose, Jeremy would have been sent to the mental hospital, the trial would have been delayed, and who knew what ugly chain of events would follow.

Did I just try to commit suicide?

He hadn't necessarily had suicidal thoughts as he tied the sheet around his neck, but had felt compelled to do something, anything to get rid of the fear that had bubbled up in his soul.

And it had worked. The shivering stopped, the disturbing thoughts of death left, and he almost felt like his normal self. Instead of doubtful thoughts plaguing his mind, he remembered Linda's last conversation with him, after the trial had ended on Friday.

"I think that was a really strong first week for us," she said. "We're in good shape going into the next two weeks, where the testimony will start to focus on your mental state."

"How was that good?"

"The prosecution came out of the gate with emotional testimony—strong testimony—and they have at least one more week of witnesses. Moving forward will be more doctors and the science behind mental health, pushing the emotional testimony further back in the jury's memory. I think Geoff actually played this wrong. He wanted to come out with a heavy punch of emotion, but now he might lose the jury to boredom. We need to capitalize on the next week and we may be able to get out of this thing alive."

"So there's no more emotional stories coming?"

"Oh, don't kid yourself, there's still more. I expect they'll end with a bang. Your old coworker, Elayna, she suffered some serious brain damage and can't speak anymore. She'll be their last witness."

Jeremy had had a good relationship with Elayna. She was a big baseball fan like him, and they would sometimes spend Friday lunch breaks at the bar next to the office, watching whatever day game might be on. It would hurt to see her in bad shape and he was glad he could brace himself for it.

"I just wanted you to know we're still in this," Linda told him. Her voice sounded fake, but Jeremy rolled with it. "Have you been paying attention to the jury at all?"

He shook his head.

"From my experience, three jurors usually decide the whole case. Three jurors pay close attention and take detailed notes throughout an entire trial, and go into deliberation to sway people to see things their way. I've seen only two jurors take heavy notes: the older woman in the first seat, and the man in the suit. I'll be focusing on these two during our cross-examinations and of course the closing statements. If we can convince them, we may be able to convince all of them."

Ms. Serious might be my savior? Who would have thought?

25

Chapter 25

Monday, October 30, 2017
  Day 6 of the trial

Clark Owen sat in the witness box, fidgeting nervously. He had never liked confrontation, or being the center of attention, so being in a witness box to testify about his old, murderous friend was worse than being buried alive.

After all this time, Clark had maintained his fiery beard, grooming it for his court appearance. Not many witnesses had been able to make eye contact with Jeremy, but Clark couldn't keep his sad brown eyes off him. Jeremy, for his part, couldn't make himself meet Clark's stare. He hadn't wanted to kill Clark that day and got lucky: he saw Clark in the parking lot before he entered the building.

Geoff opened questioning. "Mr. Owen, how long did you work with the defendant?"

"I was there before he joined the company, so I technically worked with him his entire time there," Clark said in a shy voice.

"How long did you work with him directly on the same

team?"

"For two years, up until the shooting."

"How would you describe your relationship with the defendant?"

Clark paused, staring to the ceiling in search of the right words. "We were friends. I considered him my closest friend in the office."

This statement forced Jeremy to look up to Clark, and their eyes locked immediately, causing Jeremy's stomach to flip like a gymnast.

"I find it interesting that you two were such good friends, and miraculously on the day your friend decides to shoot everyone in sight, you were nowhere to be seen. Where were you during the shooting?"

Clark shifted in his seat. "I had gone out to my car. I was trying to buy something online and couldn't find my credit card, so I went to my car to look for it."

"That's convenient." Clark looked down to his lap, his eyes bulging in shock.

Linda shook her head in disbelief. Jeremy assumed that she would have objected to his hostility, but she didn't.

"According to the police reports, and the statement you provided, you walked out of the office door where the defendant's car was parked. You would have walked right by his car on your way out, and you didn't think anything of it?"

"No, sir. I was just going to my car, I wasn't paying attention to whose car I passed."

"Did the defendant ever hint to you about what he was going to do?"

"No."

"Did he ever express his disgust toward upper management

to you?"

"Yes. We both did. We were both treated unfairly and often vented to each other."

"Ever about Shelly Williams directly?"

"Yes, of course. She was the one holding us both back."

"But never a suggestion of violence?"

"No. It was normal coworker talk about hating our boss, nothing special." Clark spoke with a hint of frustration. He seemed to want to defend Jeremy.

"Did you ever spend time with the defendant outside of work?"

"Yes. We would go to happy hours, lunch, and even golfing sometimes."

"When was the last time you had an out-of-office get-together?"

"It was the day before the shooting, March 10."

"What did you do?"

"We went to lunch near the office."

"And still no mention of any sort of planned attack, or a warning to you to keep away the following day?"

"No, sir."

"Just so I'm clear of the timeline of events." Geoff paused and flipped to a new page on his notepad. "You two would complain about Shelly from time to time. On Thursday, March 10, the day before the shooting, you and the defendant went to lunch. On Friday, March 11, the defendant goes out to his car to prepare for his shooting, and at the same time you head outside to your car to look for a credit card, and just happen to stay out there while the shooting took place inside?"

"Yes."

Linda stood slowly. "Objection?" she asked, apparently not

sure exactly what she was objecting. "Is this an interrogation or testimony?"

Judge Zamora nodded his head and put a fist to his mouth. "Mr. Batchelor, I do agree with Ms. Kennedy. Your questioning seems a bit odd. I'm going to allow the last question, but please try to keep this focused on the trial of Jeremy Heston, not Clark Owen."

Geoff replied, "Of course, Your Honor," and Linda sat down with a victorious grin.

"My apologies, Mr. Owen," Geoff said as he returned his attention to the redhead on the stand. "You never crossed paths with the defendant on the morning of March 11?"

"Correct."

"And you were never tipped off about the shooting by the defendant?"

"No."

"No more questions."

The courtroom remained silent as Geoff returned to his table. Clark's face turned a shade of pink as he waited for the defense to step up. Something felt off, and the whole courtroom could sense it.

Jeremy remembered back to the moment just before he entered the office. He had just locked the back door with the two-by-four and come running around the corner when he saw Clark disappear into the sea of cars. Clark was telling the truth.

The district attorney had tried to create a narrative that could have placed a lot of doubt in the minds of the jury, and had failed miserably.

Linda stood at the podium and flipped through her pages of notes.

"Mr. Owen, you and the defendant were friends. Good friends. Did he ever share things about his personal life with you?"

"Yes. We shared stories about our family life and our past."

"Did he ever mention to you that he owned a gun?"

"Yes, he did. He told me when he bought it. My father was a gun collector, so I've always had an interest in guns."

"When did he tell you he bought the gun?"

Clark crunched his face in thought. "It would've been late 2015, I don't remember exactly when."

"Do you own a gun?"

"Yes, I do. Just a small pistol I keep for protection."

"Did you ever go shooting with the defendant?"

"No. We talked about it, but never set the plans."

"During your time working with the defendant, did he ever show signs of violent behavior?"

"No. He was always loving and cared about the team. I'd even call him a peacekeeper, when things got out of hand."

"What do you mean by 'when things got out of hand'?"

"Well, Jeremy was just always there for us. We went through some tough times as a team when we had management change. Jeremy was always there as a voice of reason."

"What did you talk about that day before the shooting at lunch?"

"We talked about the upcoming baseball season and about work."

"What exactly about work?"

"We hadn't caught up after Jeremy was put on his PIP, so we talked about that process and how we felt our new manager, Mark, was leading us in a bad direction."

"Was a talk like this out of the norm for you two?"

"No. It was actually what we always talked about: work and sports."

"What happened when you went outside on March 11? There must have been something that told you to not go back into the building."

"Yes. I heard gunshots coming from inside as I approached the building again."

"Did you see the two-by-four that barricaded the door?"

"I did. I kept my distance though. I could hear loud screams and what sounded like banging on the walls."

"What did you do at that point?"

"I went back to my car and called the police. They told me they had already received a bunch of calls and were on the way."

"At what point did you learn that Mr. Heston was the shooter?"

"Not until I got home that evening and saw the news. Everyone I talked to that made it out alive didn't get a clear look at Jeremy. All they said was a man dressed in all black started shooting at the office."

"Thank you, Mr. Owen. No further questions."

Clark stood and walked down the center aisle, keeping his stare fixed on Jeremy. The two locked eyes one final time before Clark walked out of Jeremy's life forever.

26

Chapter 26

Monday, October 30, 2017

Jeremy remembered shooting at Melissa Marsh. She had poked her face around the corner shortly after he opened fire. His reflex in the moment was to point his AR-15 right at her and pull the trigger. She had turned to run, her long blond hair flowing behind her as she escaped.

Now she sat on the witness stand, same long hair, same big blue eyes that had bulged at the sight of the gun. Her already pale skin appeared even lighter. She seemed tense, Jeremy thought, glancing around the courtroom nervously. *You could probably use one of these pills I'm taking.*

"Ms. Marsh, when did you work at Open Hands?" Geoff asked.

"I started there in 2010, when the company was still E-Nonymous. I worked there until the shooting."

"What was your role with the company?"

"I worked on the People team. That's what we called human resources. I started as a recruiter and eventually took on more responsibilities across the H.R. spectrum."

"Did you recruit the defendant?"

She nodded her head and looked down as she spoke. "I did."

"How did your early conversations with him go?"

"They were normal recruiting conversations. He had a strong interest in joining the company, and we really loved his background. It was an easy hire for us."

"Were you ever aware that he had been fired from his previous job before joining E-Nonymous?"

"No."

"Would you have hired him if you knew that fact?"

She paused and considered the question.

"Honestly, it's hard to say. We would have asked him about it, learned the circumstance around the firing, and decided from there."

"In the four years of employment, excluding the first three months of 2016, had there ever been disciplinary action filed for the defendant?"

"Nothing ever reported to the People team, no."

"In January of 2016, the defendant was placed on what you called a performance improvement plan. Were you involved in that process at all?"

"Yes. I worked directly with Shelly Williams and Mark Fernandez, Jeremy's director and manager, on drawing up the paperwork and recording it in our system."

"Did you think anything was out of the ordinary about this disciplinary action against him?" Geoff asked.

"No. It was a standard PIP."

"Did Shelly or Mark discuss any of the matters with you before filing the PIP?"

"Yes. Shelly did. It's common for a manager to want to discuss matters before jumping to any rash decisions. Shelly had felt she was out of options after speaking with Jeremy on multiple occasions."

"Can you explain how the PIP process works once an employee is placed on it?"

"A PIP serves as a thirty-day probation period. The employee will no longer qualify for bonuses, promotions, or raises during that time period. During the thirty days the employee is expected to improve their performance based on specific metrics outlined in the PIP. If they do, they can come off it after thirty days. If they don't, then further discipline could take place, up to and including termination."

She sounds like a legal document come to life, Jeremy thought.

"And what happened in the defendant's case?" Geoff asked.

"He made drastic improvements and came off the PIP after the thirty days. All had returned to normal according to Shelly."

"So it worked then?"

"Yes, I'd say so."

"Is it true that your company conducted its review process around this same time?"

"Yes."

"How did that factor in with regard to the defendant?"

"The reviews occurred while he was on the PIP. He was denied a raise with the stipulation that we would have another review with him at the end of summer."

"Was that stipulation normal?"

"No. We wanted to give him a fair shot, since the timing didn't work out in his favor. He had been with the company for so long and was still highly valued."

"So the company wanted to take care of him despite all of this," Geoff said, more to himself than to her. "Were you also involved in the process of terminating his employment in

March?"

"Yes."

"Tell us what happened, please."

"There was an incident where an employee on Jeremy's team went to Shelly to complain about some things Jeremy had said about her."

"Janae Ortiz?"

"Yes. Jeremy had apparently been gossiping about Janae when he thought she wasn't around. She went to Shelly, and Shelly became fed up with giving Jeremy more chances. It was the last straw for her."

"And it was at this point she filed the paperwork to terminate his employment?"

"Yes."

"Do you recall the date of his termination?"

"March 11, 2016."

"We all know what happened on that day instead. Thank you for your time, Ms. Marsh."

Geoff stepped away from the podium with a confident swagger.

Linda stood and walked slowly to the podium as she shuffled a stack of papers.

"Good afternoon, Ms. Marsh. I don't have too many questions for you today. First off, is it normal for managers to warn an employee that they might be fired?"

Linda had come out with the hard punch she wanted, and Melissa was taken aback. "I'm not sure what you mean," she replied in a soft voice.

"The events leading up to the day have been heavily discussed. One thing that's been consistent throughout is the fact that Shelly Williams pulled Jeremy Heston into a conference room on March 10 and warned him he might be fired. Is that normal?" Linda spoke in a condescending voice.

"Well, no."

"Is it normal to take an employee's word regarding another employee's actions without conducting some sort of investigation?"

"No."

"Was there any investigation by the People team into the gossiping of which my client was accused?"

"No."

"Then why was the next step in the process to jump to termination?"

"Jeremy had just come off a PIP. Also, Colorado is an at-will state, meaning we can terminate anyone's employment without any reason." Melissa had returned with some sass, but her attempt enraged Linda.

"Thank you, Ms. Marsh, I know the employment laws in the state I've been practicing in for the last two decades." Linda raised a thick stack of papers. "This is the official company guidelines for Open Hands, Incorporated. Section four, article three says that any employee undergoing disciplinary action should first be placed on a Performance Improvement Plan so long as their offense is not extreme."

"Correct."

"I didn't ask you anything. Have you ever read this document?"

Melissa slunk back in her seat. "Yes, of course." Her voice had the shamed pitch of defeat.

"I've learned a lot about the Open Hands company. To me they seem like a very fair, fun, and levelheaded to company to work for. Would you agree?"

"Yes."

"Then I want to know why this one instance was not handled fairly. Accusing someone of gossip is not grounds for termination in most companies. Especially after no investigation. Your team didn't even talk to Jeremy about the incident. You just took someone's word on the matter and made a very rash decision afterward. Did the events of March 10 go as they normally would have for any other employee?"

"I don't know." Melissa voice had shrunk into shame.

"How convenient. No more questions."

Linda glided back to her seat with a wide smile that sent chills down Jeremy's spine. A juror's jaw hung open. His attorney was batshit crazy and he loved it.

27

Chapter 27

Tuesday, October 31, 2017
Day 7 of the trial

The second week of the trial brought more nostalgia for Jeremy. Seeing Clark had sparked a flood of memories and Halloween morning brought another blast to the past, when he saw the man who had indirectly sparked this whole thing.

Dr. Siva sat in the box, broad-shouldered and confident. The last eighteen months had aged him, and white had started to replace the gray. Jeremy's old mentor kept his eyes on him much like Clark had, but this time Jeremy *wanted* to meet his stare.

"Dr. Siva, how do you know the defendant?" Geoff asked.

"I'm a professor at Denver State University. Mr. Heston was one of my students."

"I understand that you had a closer relationship with the defendant than with most of your students."

"Correct. Mr. Heston and I met every month at my office, to catch up on life—and his coursework, when school was in session."

"So you met with him even when school wasn't in session?"

"Yes, sir."

"Why?"

"When I first met Jeremy outside of class, he had come by with a question on an assigned paper. Talking with him showed me he had a bright future as a psychologist. It was a hunch, but you can always tell the special students apart."

"What sparked the monthly meetings?"

"After our first meeting, I asked him to drop back in after he had completed the assignment. I wanted to know what he had come up with."

"What was the assignment?"

"It was a high-level assignment where the students could write about any topic as long as it related to mental health. Mr. Heston chose to write about the effects of schizophrenia."

"Did you know he had a family member that suffered from the disease?"

"Not at the time, but I did learn that later on."

"How many students have you had monthly meetings with throughout your career as a professor?"

Dr. Siva bobbed his head side to side as he mentally counted them. "There have been eight others that I can recall."

"So it's not a common occurrence?"

"Not at all. I like to connect with my highly talented students and guide them throughout this field. It's competitive and complex to get started in a career as a psychologist or psychiatrist."

"How did these conversations go with the defendant?"

"When he started his initial job after obtaining his bachelor's degree, I warned him of the corporate world potentially being a roadblock in his path as a psychologist. He loved the company so much though, it didn't resonate with him until later."

"Did he ever discuss his director, Shelly Williams, with you?"

"Yes, he did. In the months leading up to this attack, her name started to come up, but it wasn't anything that would suggest such a violent outburst."

"What did he say about her?"

"All he ever mentioned was how she held him back, turned him down at every opportunity that arose. Things happened exactly as I feared they would; she crushed his high hopes."

"You said you try to guide your special students to careers in psychology. How did you do this with the defendant?"

"I saw my younger self in him. I encouraged him to think big, think of ways to change the world. Maybe he could have found the cure to something. Now we'll never know."

Jeremy's gut twisted into hard knots. He had always wanted to tell Dr. Siva that this was all a big experiment to shed light on mental health, but he knew that the less his professor knew the better off they both would be.

"Dr. Siva, I know you never had formal interviews with the defendant, like the other doctors in this trial, but in your professional opinion did the defendant ever show signs of mental illness?"

Dr. Siva paused and scratched his head with dry, cracked fingers.

"Schizophrenia is very much hereditary. I never personally saw signs, but then again, I only had an hour each month to really talk with Jeremy."

"No further questions."

Fuck, Jeremy thought. That last statement could come back to haunt him. If the person closest to Jeremy—in the psychology field—wouldn't testify to his insanity, how could he expect the verdict to be any different?

Wilbert rose immediately as Geoff turned away from the podium, wasting no time beginning his cross-examination.

"Dr. Siva, you spent a lot of time with Mr. Heston over the two years before the shooting. Would you say it's possible you may have not noticed signs of a dormant mental illness?"

"It's very possible, yes. Though as a psychologist, you constantly study people in your life to see what makes them tick."

"Dr. Siva, you created a notion in Jeremy's mind that the corporate world would fail him. You sat back and watched as he came in each month and told you how poorly he was being treated. Did you ever talk with him about other employment options?"

"Of course. I told him I had connections if he wanted to work in the field. I also encouraged him to consider opening a practice of his own."

"And when Mr. Heston expressed no desire to do these things, it must have upset you, right?"

"It didn't upset me. To each their own. Jeremy was a bright student and I wanted to present him with multiple options. I assumed he'd be fine with whatever route he took."

"Have you ever studied the effects of environmental factors on mental health?"

"Yes, of course."

"Then you should know that events like what happened to Mr. Heston—the constant rejection, the letdown—could have caused him to have an outburst like this."

"Yes, it's very possible. It could have started with depression and escalated. Again, I didn't have the chance to examine Jeremy. He could have easily hid his depression during the hour each month when we met."

"No further questions."

Holy shit! Jeremy thought. He wanted to stand and applaud his defense attorney. Wilbert had planted seeds of doubt. Even though Dr. Siva wasn't on the stand as a psychiatrist, Wilbert had found a way to weave in his expertise and explore the possibility of a wavering mental state.

Wilbert returned to their table with a stern face as Dr. Siva walked slowly from the witness stand.

28

Chapter 28

Thursday, November 2, 2017
  Day 9 of the trial

The days after Dr. Siva's testimony had included more testimony from some of Jeremy's old coworkers, but no one he gave a shit about.

Linda warned him of a grand finale of sorts as the prosecution neared its end of witnesses. Dr. Reed and Elayna were set as the two final witnesses. She had also informed Jeremy that the defense's lone witness, Dr. Brown, was prepared and ready to go for her testimony.

Jeremy didn't believe enough had been done to create a case for insanity. He felt helpless, stranded on an island of bickering attorneys, a hard-ass judge, and a simple-minded jury. The only way off the island was to pray to God that something would resonate with the jurors, to allow them to see things the way his fucked-up mind did.

Am I really insane?

Jeremy had considered it before, but never took the thought seriously. Did insane people know they were insane? He was on pills after all, and two doctors agreed that he suffered from mental insanity. Schizophrenia pumped in his veins.

Nah. I'm not crazy.

Jeremy refused to believe he was anything other than a normal man figuring out life in his twenties. He had suffered heartbreak, rejection, friendships falling apart, and he had dealt with it.

This was all a planned experiment from the beginning. Planned to the finest detail, up to and during the day of the shooting. Everything after that was in God's hands.

Crazy people don't make plans.

The time in jail was finally getting to him. He'd been having conversations with himself lately, but didn't think much of it. Who the fuck else was he supposed to talk to?

"We call Dr. William Reed to the stand," Geoff said, interrupting Jeremy's internal debate.

Dr. Reed strolled to the witness stand with slouched shoulders and a wide grin. *Clearly not his first court appearance,* Jeremy thought.

Dr. Reed wore a pinstriped suit, shiny black shoes, and a flashy Rolex. The jurors gawked at him.

"Dr. Reed, good morning and welcome," Geoff said.

"Good morning, Mr. Batchelor."

Jeremy had the feeling he was about to get fucked in the ass by this hotshot psychiatrist and the district attorney.

"Can you please tell the jury your background?"

"I've worked as a forensic psychologist for the last twenty years. I also have my PhD and am a practicing psychiatrist back home, when I'm not working on a case."

"How many criminal cases have you worked on?"

"Over one hundred. I've honestly lost count."

"Can you tell us about the extensive interview process? What did it consist of?"

"The interview process is designed to learn about the defendant, from the time of early childhood all the way up to the present day. The questions are designed to identify certain behavioral patterns from each time frame in his life. We look at how those patterns could have changed over time based on environmental factors."

"What did you find when working with the defendant?"

"I conducted over twenty hours of interviews with the defendant, within a month of the crime he committed, along with some follow-up meetings leading up to this trial. I believe that the defendant is mentally ill, but was legally sane at the time of the shooting."

Jeremy shot a look at Linda, who avoided eye contact and wrote on her notepad with a tight-lipped smile. *Mentally ill but legally sane? What kind of crock of shit is that?*

"What was your initial diagnosis?"

"I found the defendant to have schizotypal personality disorder. This is a disorder that is characterized by severe social anxiety and can include paranoia and hallucinations."

"Now, you mentioned that the defendant is mentally ill, but legally sane. Can you elaborate on what that means exactly?"

"Yes. Under the legal system, someone being considered insane implies that they either did not know what they were doing, or they were unable to decipher the difference between right and wrong."

"And you believe that the defendant acted *not* under either of those conditions?"

"Correct. The schizotypal disorder would have affected him in a way that made him awkward in social settings, but would not have clouded his judgment. He knew what he was doing and he knew it was wrong."

Geoff paused his questioning, wanting that last statement to hang in the air as long as possible. This was his moment to win over the jury and he had to play each move to perfection.

"Dr. Reed, have you found this disorder to be something that is present all throughout life, or can it be developed over time?"

"Both. A person can be born with this disorder and grow up socially awkward. A person can also develop it later, because of environmental factors in their life."

"Such as?"

"While it's not common, it can develop from neglect and abuse. Rejection from society can also cue a person to adjust their outlook on life."

"Do you believe the defendant developed this later in life or had it since birth?"

"The defendant's great-grandfather suffered from schizophrenia, meaning schizophrenia is more likely to be inherited at some point down the line. Our final conclusion was that he has always had this disorder, but his positive upbringing and childhood never allowed it to have its typical effects. The disorder would have been dormant over the years, but his repetitive rejection could have easily woken it."

"Which rejections are you referring to specifically?"

"The end of his romantic relationship after four years, and the repeated rejection in the workplace. It created a perfect storm."

Jeremy watched the exchange continue back and forth, stunned as he saw what remained of his life flash by. Dr. Reed knew exactly what to say. He described his findings scientifically and immediately translated them to layperson's terms for the jury.

Geoff and Dr. Reed carried on as gracefully as two friends catching up after time apart. Their confidence radiated throughout the courtroom.

Jeremy imagined being strapped to a gurney, an IV inserted into his arm as he awaited the sweet poison of death to fill his body. The two men's voices drifted into background noise as he felt the room start to spin around him. He closed his eyes to try and gather himself and snapped out of it when Linda nudged him as she stood up.

All eyes were on the district attorney and the doctor as they completed their chat.

"Thank you, Dr. Reed," Geoff said, his voice heartfelt.

"My pleasure," the doctor replied.

Linda approached the podium and cleared her throat. Her hands trembled slightly, Jeremy could see—she knew this cross-examination would be instrumental in deciding the trial. They had decided before the trial that Linda would handle the technical witnesses, while Wilbert would cross-examine the emotional witnesses to play to his strengths as the storyteller.

"Good morning, Dr. Reed." Linda needed to take a strong approach out of the gate. "I think your statements contradict themselves. You state that the defendant has had this mental illness throughout his whole life, but it remained hidden until negative events happened. Then all of a sudden he's not mentally ill on the day of the shooting?"

"No, ma'am. I stated that he is mentally ill, but legally sane. He could still decipher right from wrong. What he did was wrong and he knew it."

"I see. Dr. Reed, how common is the schizotypal personality disorder?"

"It's not common. It occurs in roughly three percent of the population."

"Is this disorder something you've come across in your decades of work in this field?"

"I have dealt with this disorder a couple times before, yes."

"Was it in a criminal setting like this?"

"One case was; the other was clinical, in my practice."

"Is it possible to suffer from this disorder and not have violent outbursts?"

"Yes, it is. This disorder starts more as depression and can remain in that stage for quite some time."

"After reading your diagnosis a few months ago I did some reading on this disorder. Correct me if I'm wrong, but I understand that people with this disorder have trouble maintaining close relationships with those around them, due to fear that others are having negative thoughts about them. Paranoia, right?"

"Correct."

"They also avoid forming new relationships altogether, is that correct?"

"Correct."

"Well, Dr. Reed, I believe there are some flaws in your diagnosis. Mr. Heston never exhibited trouble maintaining relationships."

"I disagree. He lost all contact with his girlfriend." Dr. Reed took a combative tone with Linda.

"That's true, but that's life. Friendships and relationships end every day. People grow apart, especially after high school and college—which is exactly what happened here."

The jury watched the exchange like a tennis match, moving their heads from Linda to Dr. Reed as they each spoke.

"Dr. Reed, I would never discredit your work. You're as good as it gets in this field, but something is just not adding up for me. The defendant has a track record of being loved by his peers in the office, and interacted with the entire team quite often. I fully support that my client is suffering from a mental illness, but not from schizotypal personality disorder. The traits you mention don't add up with the whole story."

Go get him, Linda.

Dr. Reed hesitated a moment. "I stand by my diagnosis. The symptoms aren't one-size-fits-all. Mr. Heston could have gone on every day at work as if everything were fine. A mental illness can affect parts of the brain and have minimal visible signs. Just like if you get the sniffles in the winter, but don't develop a full cold. The human body fights illnesses, and the mind is no different."

Linda glanced to Wilbert, who was sitting on the edge of his seat, then she flipped a few pages ahead in her notes.

"Dr. Reed, you've testified in 127 trials before today, and in 102 of those trials you were testifying on behalf of a prosecution against an insanity plea. Does that sound correct?"

"OBJECTION!" Geoff barked, saliva flying from his lips.

"Overruled!" Judge Zamora snapped back without missing a beat. "Answer the question, Dr. Reed."

"Yes, that sounds correct."

Linda walked in front of the podium, taking a power pose as she stepped closer to Dr. Reed. Wilbert sat further forward, nodding his head as his partner went in for the kill.

"Of those 102 defendants you testified as being legally sane, did you know thirteen of them have been treated by your own hospital? And ten others have since been diagnosed as having very serious mental illnesses that required immediate medical treatment?"

"OBJECTION!" Geoff begged.

"Overruled! Dr. Reed?"

"I didn't know of this. I don't follow up with defendants after the trials end."

"Okay, but there's still the thirteen in your very hospital, all of whom were prescribed medication. Do you know the doctor who signed off on those prescriptions?"

Dr. Reed looked down, his bald head glowing under the bright lights, beads of sweat starting to form. "I'm the only one who signs off on prescriptions in my hospital."

"I see. So how much money did Mr. Batchelor offer you to testify against this defendant?"

"OBJECTION!" Geoff's face turned bright red. *Easy, Mr. Batchelor, the blood might start seeping out of your pores.*

"Sustained," Judge Zamora replied.

"No further questions, thank you for your time today." Linda turned and walked away from the podium with her head high. If she'd had a microphone, Jeremy thought, she would have dropped it. She'd accomplished what she set out to: planting a seed of doubt about Dr. Reed's credibility. The cross-examination had been a victory.

Jeremy looked across to Geoff and saw him furiously flipping through his notepad, his face turning purple like a plum.

"Let's break for lunch and reconvene at 1 p.m. for the next witness," Judge Zamora said, excusing everyone from the courtroom.

The gallery broke out in frantic discussion about what they had just witnessed. Linda had just called out the prosecution's biggest witness as a fraud, and the district attorney could do nothing but sit there and take it.

The seed of doubt has been planted, Jeremy thought. *It's game time.*

29

Chapter 29

November 2, 2017, 5 p.m.

"How on Earth did you do that?" Wilbert asked. They'd returned to the offices of Kennedy, Dobbs, and Irvine after court. The team back at the office buzzed with excitement after watching Linda do the impossible: discrediting the prosecution's main witness.

"Did you see how red Batchelor turned?" an assistant cackled. "He looked like his head was gonna pop!"

As they all shared a laugh, Linda was reminded that this truly was a team effort. Her team did the heavy lifting: compiling evidence, looking for any flaw in the opposition's witnesses.

Wilbert sat in the seat across Linda's desk. "I feel we have a huge advantage in this trial right now. Batchelor completely dropped the ball on Heston's friend, Clark, and now this show you put on today with Dr. Reed. How did you find that stuff out? There's no way any of that was public information."

Linda crossed her office and closed the door before returning to her desk, where she stood and faced out the window. "We have someone on the inside," she said for the first time out loud, letting the words hang in the air so she could contemplate them.

"Who? What do you mean?" Wilbert sat forward in his chair.

"I honestly don't know."

Linda sat down in her chair and pulled open a drawer. She retrieved a large manila envelope and dropped it on the desk in front of Wilbert, pointing to it like it was poisoned.

"I have no idea where that came from," she said. "It came in with my mail. No note, no return address, nothing."

Wilbert pulled the contents out of the envelope, a stack of about a hundred pieces of paper. Flipping through them, he found court documents from Dr. Reed's past testimony in different trials, along with corresponding documents show-ing the admission and medication information for the same patients admitted to his hospital.

"What in the world?" Wilbert uttered under his breath as he flipped through the pages. "Has there been anything else?"

Linda nodded, and Wilbert stood and walked to her desk.

"Another envelope just like this came through a few months ago, with a list of all the jurors who had been summoned. Every last one of them. There was a check next to every person who was supposedly a good fit, along with notes on their views on the death penalty."

Wilbert shook his head. "I don't get it," he said, dropping the envelope and papers on her desk. "Who could pull this off? And why?"

"I thought it might be his parents, seeing as they seem to have money to throw around for this trial. I had a friend run a background check for me, and their bank records don't show enough money to cover something like this. The strange thing too is they don't have the money in their accounts that they've been paying us with. Maybe they stash their cash in the mattress, but I just don't know."

"Something's going on. Very suspicious. Why didn't you tell me about any of this?"

"I didn't know how you'd react. It's a gray area. I didn't do anything illegal, this stuff just showed up and I used it to our advantage."

"It is shady, but if we have someone trying to help us win this case, I see no reason not to use the resources provided." Wilbert continued to shake his head in disbelief. "Linda, this is all lining up as a once in a lifetime opportunity. And you're front and center. Whoever your friend is, they're going to change your life. Hell, they already have. You destroying that poor doctor on the stand is going to be all over the news. I hope you're ready for stardom."

"Please, there's no such thing as famous lawyers."

"Johnny Cochran was plenty famous, and he lived a luxurious life because of it."

"He also fought for civil rights."

"You don't think that's what you're doing now? Fighting for the rights of the mentally ill?"

Linda considered this.

"That's exactly what you're doing," Wilbert said without letting her respond. "There's an entire community of mental health advocates following this trial, and they all want to see Heston receive an insanity verdict. It's happened before, but never on such a grand stage."

"I never looked at it that way," Linda said. She'd grown so focused on how the trial would help her career that she never considered the implications it could have on the rest of the country watching. "I don't know why this is all happening,"

Linda said as she pulled the manila envelope back to herself. "Something about this trial just feels *off.*"

"No shit. You have a mystery person trying to fix the outcome—or at least heavily influence it. Who knows what else they're doing behind the scenes."

"What do we do?"

"We don't do anything. We keep using what they're sending us and move forward. Business as usual. Clearly the person is on our side. I don't see any curveballs coming from the D.A. Let's just keep this between us and there shouldn't be any issues."

"I need a drink." Linda placed the envelope back in her drawer and pulled out a bottle of scotch and two glasses. "You're gonna need some, too."

30

Chapter 30

Friday, November 3, 2017
  Day 10 of the trial

Friday marked the final day of the prosecution's case before turning it over to the defense. Jeremy finished his breakfast and was led into the courtroom shortly after. He knew who the next witness was and wished he could hide. He'd never wanted his friends to suffer.

Everyone rose as Judge Zamora entered the courtroom. "Mr. Batchelor, you may call your next witness," he said after he sat.

Geoff approached the podium. "Your Honor, we call Elayna Avery to the stand."

Geoff pulled the wooden podium aside, clearing space in the aisle, and turned to the back of the courtroom, where two people stood pushing a blond woman in a wheelchair.

Jeremy turned to look. The woman who pushed Elayna in the wheelchair resembled her; he assumed it was her mother. Another woman trailed them, dressed in a business suit and carrying a large white board with the letters of the alphabet splayed across it.

Elayna was pushed to the witness stand, her arms gripping the side bars of her wheelchair and her stare fixed straight ahead. She looked past Jeremy, but he could see the hole where her right eye used to be.

"Mr. Batchelor, it's my understanding that Ms. Avery is unable to physically speak, correct?" Judge Zamora asked.

"Yes, Your Honor. We have Ms. Sterling from the state here to relay the witness's testimony."

"Very well." Judge Zamora turned to the woman called Mrs. Sterling. "Ms. Sterling, I need to administer an oath to you. Please raise your right hand."

Ms. Sterling rose a skinny arm in the air.

"Do you solemnly swear and affirm under the penalty of law that you will accurately, impartially, and to the best of your abilities verbalize the answers of this witness?"

"I do."

Judge Zamora turned to Elayna, now in the witness box and looking at the judge.

"Ms. Avery, do you solemnly swear that your testimony today will contain the truth, the whole truth, and nothing but the truth?"

"Ahhhhhh oooooh," Elayna responded in a mumble. Jeremy's heart ached. Despite her eye, which looked like a smashed mass of flesh, Elayna looked mostly herself. She wore a long, green dress that sparkled in the light, and had her once long blond hair cut to shoulder length.

Jeremy played back the day of March 11 in his mind and couldn't recall shooting Elayna specifically. He remembered her shivering on the ground, though. He had assumed she would eventually pass on, but apparently she'd had the fight to keep going.

"Good morning, ma'am," Geoff said from the pushed-aside podium. "Can you please spell your first name for the record?"

Elayna pointed at the big white board that had been placed in front of her and started jumping from letter to letter.

"E-L-A-Y-N-A," Mrs. Sterling spoke from over Elayna's shoulder.

"Were you in the Open Hands office on March 11, 2016?"

"Y-E-S," Mrs. Sterling said as Elayna again pointed to the letters.

"No further questions, Your Honor."

That's it? Did he just use Elayna as an emotional pawn for the jury? Jeremy thought, fuming at the idea.

"Ms. Kennedy, any questions for the witness?"

"No, Your Honor," Linda said as she stood and sat back down quickly.

"Thank you, Ms. Avery, you are excused," Judge Zamora said to Elayna.

"Uhhhhhhh," she moaned.

Fuck, Jeremy thought. Elayna would be disabled the rest of her life. Why couldn't she have just let go? He remembered the police officer who testified about saving Elayna, her bleeding out in the backseat, and wondered how someone could actually will themselves to live. He wasn't surprised to learn that Elayna had been the fighter to make it through, considering she had always strived to be the best on the team.

A bullet had gone through her eye, taking chunks of brain with it on the way out, and she still managed to live.

God bless her.

Jeremy felt tears welling in his eyes and blinked them out before anyone noticed.

Elayna's mother returned and pushed Elayna out of the

courtroom, Ms. Sterling trailing behind them once again. Geoff held open the gate for them and repositioned the podium once they exited.

"Mr. Batchelor, your next witness please," the judge said.

"Your Honor, the prosecution rests."

Cameras clicked in excitement from the single row of press and a murmur spread throughout the courtroom. Phase one of the trial was complete—things would start moving quickly now that they had made it through the prosecution's laundry list of witnesses.

It hit Jeremy like an uppercut to the chin: by the following week, the rest of his life could very well be decided.

"Ladies and gentlemen," Judge Zamora said. "With the prosecution resting their case, I propose we adjourn court until Monday. Any oppositions to that from counsel?" Linda and Geoff shook their heads. "Very well. Ladies and gentlemen of the jury, there will be a lot of press coverage of the trial this weekend, so I'll remind you to avoid the television and any conversation surrounding this trial. With the prosecution finished, please bear in mind that they have the burden of proving the defendant was sane during the time of attack. Next week you'll hear from the defense's witnesses before we conclude for deliberation. Any questions?"

The jurors looked around at each other, shaking their heads

"Thank you, and have a pleasant weekend. Court is adjourned."

The banging of the gavel echoed throughout the room, and it sounded crisper to Jeremy than any time before.

The audience broke into immediate chatter, and if Jeremy had turned around he would have seen a handful of people in tears from Elayna's testimony. His parents sat in the front row, as they had all trial, but he didn't so much as glance in their direction. Linda had told him he was doing a good job in court showing no emotions, so despite his wanting to break down on the inside, he saved that for when the lights went out in his jail cell.

The image of Elayna's empty eye socket would forever burn in his mind, and he accepted that.

31

Chapter 31

Monday, November 6, 2017
  Day 11 of the trial

On Monday morning the courtroom hummed with energy. Word had leaked over the weekend that the defense only had one witness to call, which meant deliberations would start this afternoon.

Jeremy was pleased to hear that media coverage had increased over the weekend and many outlets had made plans to cover the verdict reading live.

Linda had visited him on Saturday to update him on the next steps. There wasn't much he didn't already know. After the defense rested their case and closing statements were completed, he would simply wait until the jury returned with a verdict. The waiting game could range anywhere from a few hours to a few days, possibly even a few weeks. It all depended on how the jury felt right off the bat. If most were leaning one way, it could be a quick process to persuade the remaining few to vote in their favor. If the jury was split, then they could expect to wait a while.

"Quick never acquits," she said. "We'll know by the end of Tuesday how this might look. Hopefully. Another thing to keep in mind is that juries usually make the same decision the judge would. Even though the judge has no official vote, listen closely to how he presents the jury with their final instructions. His tone will be slanted one way or another. I'm gonna be listening for how much emphasis he puts on the fact that the prosecution has the burden of proof for your sanity."

"So when do you think we'll know?"

"Hard to say. This has been a tough jury to read, partly because of how long the trial has been. People tend to lose the enthusiasm they might have had for a typical three-day trial, and just want to go home and get back to their lives. Closing statements will conclude Monday afternoon. The jury will come back early Tuesday morning to start deliberation. I'd say if we don't hear anything by two o'clock, things will be looking favorable. If they turn in a decision before then, I'm afraid it won't be one you'll want to hear."

Jeremy kept this in mind as his guts bubbled in angst on Monday morning. Within the next two weeks, at most, his life would be decided. He would either succeed in his mission for the mentally ill or would have to suffer the rest of his days wondering what the fuck went wrong. If convicted, he would become a mere footnote in history. People would talk about him in social gatherings years from now and say how they wished someone would just off him in prison already and stop wasting the taxpayers' money. Or there was still the chance that they'd call for the death penalty and put him out of his misery. Jeremy wasn't sure which would be worse.

"I think his name started with a J," they'd say as he sat every day looking at the wall and waiting for the reaper to come pick him up.

Judge Zamora entered to begin the final day of testimony.

"All rise!" the bailiff barked from his corner. Judge Zamora hurried to his bench and everyone sat in unison, seats creaking as all chatter ceased.

"Good morning, folks," the judge greeted them. "Ms. Kennedy, it's my understanding you will call one witness today, is that correct?"

"Yes, Your Honor," Linda said. She wore a strong perfume that reminded Jeremy of the scent Jamie used to leave on his bedsheets.

"Mr. Batchelor, will you be ready for closing statements this afternoon?"

"Yes, Your Honor."

"Ms. Kennedy, will you be ready to follow Mr. Batchelor?"

"Yes, Your Honor."

"Very well, does counsel have anything to discuss before we call in the jury?"

"No, Your Honor," Geoff and Linda said.

Judge Zamora gestured to the bailiff to bring in the jury, and they all walked in their usual single file line to the jury box. Jeremy thought they all looked refreshed after the weekend, and he could hope that only a limited amount of the graphic crime description remained in their heads.

"Okay, Ms. Kennedy, please call your witness."

Wilbert approached the podium. They had decided he would examine their lone witness to allow Linda to save her energy for closing statements. Wilbert wore an all-black suit and looked more like Secret Service detail than a defense attorney.

"The defense calls Dr. Ana Brown."

All heads turned to the tall, slender woman walking down

the aisle. She crossed the bar and pushed her shoulder-length brown hair behind her ears. She smiled at the judge, revealing pearly teeth nearly as white as her pale skin, as she was sworn in.

"Good morning," she responded in a gentle tone to Wilbert.

Jeremy noticed the entire jury sat on the edge of their seats. They had also been informed of the upcoming timeline by the jury commissioner and knew this would be the final testimony before moving on to the next phase.

"Dr. Brown, can you please tell us about your background in psychology?"

"I attended U.C.L.A and earned my bachelor's, master's, and PhD in psychology. I have worked both as a professor and in the field of forensic psychology."

"Have you done any courtroom testimony?"

"Yes. Most of my field work has been in the criminal justice system." She spoke softly, yet confidently.

Wilbert walked her through more background questions, and she explained her process for conducting the interviews with Jeremy, similar to Dr. Reed's methods described the previous week.

"Can you please tell us your diagnosis for Mr. Heston?"

"After all my research, I believe that Mr. Heston is suffering from bipolar disorder."

Someone in the gallery gasped. So far, the only diagnoses that had been discussed were possible schizophrenia and schizotypal disorders.

"Can you tell the jury how bipolar disorder differentiates from the schizotypal disorder that Dr. Reed had diagnosed?"

"Schizotypal disorder is a sub phenotype of schizophrenia. This disorder may cause delusions or hallucinations, voices in the head, and can't be swayed. Whereas bipolar disorder causes drastic mood swings."

"And you are aware that Mr. Heston has schizophrenia in his genetics?"

"Yes."

"And you still don't believe there's a chance he's suffering from schizophrenia?"

"No. Genetics get tricky. We understand them to an extent. It's possible for bipolar disorder to work its way down the genetic line, but genes can't be given full credit for causing it. "

"Please tell us about the symptoms of bipolar disorder."

"Symptoms can vary widely, based on which mood the personality is currently in. If one is having a high, they may be extremely active in goal-oriented activities, have increased libido, racing thoughts, and a desire to spend money. If they are on the low end of the spectrum, they will show changes in appetite, sleep patterns, loss of interest in previously enjoyed activities, and a sense of worthlessness. In the most extreme cases, suicide is likely."

"I'd like for you to explain this spectrum of emotions for the jury. We have a chart you provided, so you can explain with visuals."

Wilbert pointed a remote at the same screen Geoff had shown the gory images on during opening statements, and it flicked to life with a line graph that had different colored lines going in all sorts of directions. The vertical axis was labeled from top to bottom: Mania, Hypomania, Mood, Depression.

The horizontal axis started in the middle where *Mood* was listed and ran across as a timeline of two years.

"Proceed, Dr. Brown."

"If you will first note the green line on the graph. This line represents the average person. You'll see it mostly hovers above the mood line, meaning people are generally in a positive mood. Also note it dips below the mood line to represent the lows people encounter in life. Lows typically come after job loss or a family death, for example.

"The purple line you see represents people with bipolar one disorder. Bipolar one is the most severe case of the disorder. You see how the lows dip all the way to the bottom of the graph, and the highs reach the top. The highs and lows can last anywhere from two weeks to several months at a time. The lows are a deep depression, where the person may have big changes in their sleep patterns, their appetite, and their overall joy in life. Whereas the highs can cause racing thoughts, quick speech, increased libido, and irresponsibility with decisions.

"Lastly, the blue line you see represents people with bipolar two disorder, a less severe case, where you'll see the highs and lows are about half that of bipolar one, but they still rise and fall over time."

"Thank you, Doctor," Wilbert said. "Can you explain where Mr. Heston falls into this graph, based on your diagnosis?"

"I believe Mr. Heston is suffering from bipolar one disorder. I feel he was suffering from a manic high that eventually sunk to a low that led to the events on March 11."

"I know you've given us a general outline on how this works, but please tell us what symptoms you feel applied directly to Mr. Heston."

"Of course. It's first important to note that a manic high, or manic episode, can last for several months. Looking at the big picture and the timeline of events leading up to March 11, it's fairly straightforward to see his high and also see when it started its downward trend on this graph. Focusing on the year before the shooting, Mr. Heston was very much on a high. He had a great deal of respect at his job and was in line to do big things in the future—which made him feel good. However, where most people might simply feel happy about this, those with bipolar one disorder feel their highs in the extreme.

"Mr. Heston was in a relationship at the time, and according to the interviews I conducted with him, he craved sex more than one normally would. Fortunately, Mr. Heston had other good things going on in life, such as a raise and bonus he had received from his company. Had he not had these other highs, I believe his sexual tension would have boiled to a point that sent his mood into a low. Instead, we see Mr. Heston doing other activities that would suggest a manic episode. He bought a $700 rifle—which I highly doubt he had any ill intentions for at the time of his purchase. This is where we see irresponsible spending from Mr. Heston. Aside from buying the firearm, he started clearing out his bank account every payday. According to Mr. Heston, this money was spent on strippers, alcohol, cannabis, and gambling. Assuming that is true, Mr. Heston could have maintained his high much longer than normal, as his brain became used to the increase in dopamine.

"In the fall of 2015 is where we see Mr. Heston's mood start its downward trend. But the mood doesn't change overnight. It could take weeks or months to fall from the high to a low. In the fall, Mr. Heston dealt with the rejection of a promotion and the ending of his long-term relationship, followed by another rejected promotion opportunity—three negative events that literally pulled him from his high. Where most people would fall into a slight depression for a few days after going through something like this, for someone with bipolar disorder the low would be the drastic dip you see on the graph.

"This low is considered a depressive episode, where the person can suffer from a lack of appetite, insomnia, fatigue, guilt, rage, hate, and even delusions. Mr. Heston would have started his descent to this stage in the fall and would have likely been at his lowest point during December or January. Mr. Heston did not speak fondly of his family or the holidays, compared to the way he did earlier in life. This tells me he was definitely in the midst of a depressive episode around that time, before things started to peak again around early February."

"Dr. Brown, excuse my interruption, but if Mr. Heston was trending back up by February, how does that explain the shooting a few weeks later?"

"I would call it the perfect storm. There is something within the realm of bipolar disorders called mixed affective state. This state of mind, as suggested by its name, occurs when elements of both mania and depression are present—one is having highs and lows at the same time. The mind essentially has a battle with itself, and this leaves a person to suffer from suicidal thoughts, mood swings, or trouble with impulse control."

"And you found this to be the case with Mr. Heston?"

"I did. It appeared he was on his way up from his low when he was delivered news about not receiving a raise. I feel this event triggered another downward spiral, when his mind was on its upswing. When a person enters the mixed affective state they become highly unpredictable and can find themselves going to bed happy one night and waking up with angry thoughts in the morning. At this point in time, decisions are made on a whim, with no regard for the consequences, and that's what I believe happened."

"Thank you for your time, Dr. Brown. I have no further

questions."

Wilbert returned to the table, and Jeremy could see that sheer joy hid underneath his composed façade.

Geoff approached the podium. "Hello, Dr. Brown. I feel like the genetics analysis of your case study was brushed over briefly. Can you go into the details of how the defendant could have had bipolar disorder if his ancestor had schizophrenia?"

"Schizophrenia and bipolar disorder are both mental illnesses. Both have similar characteristics of delusions and impulses. It has been proven that mental illness can be passed down through genetics, and not necessarily in the same form. Schizophrenia can easily be passed down into a form of bipolar disorder through genetics, and vice versa."

Dr. Brown spoke in a calm, defensive voice.

"Okay. Were there ever signs of bipolar disorder in the defendant's childhood?"

"Not that I found. But, bipolar disorder is a disease that can remain dormant until the age of 25. It's an illness that typically doesn't show signs until the brain is fully developed, whereas schizophrenia can begin from birth and progress with someone through their early years into adulthood."

"At any point in your interviews did you consider that all these events just happened to revolve around Shelly Williams and that this may have been an act of revenge?"

"Of course. I never rule out any possibility until there is a clear answer. While Mr. Heston's case can appear to be an act of revenge, there were many external factors as well that contributed to his actions. Shelly Williams was simply another one of those factors."

"So you admit his actions can appear to be an act of revenge?"

"Yes, they can appear so, but looking into the matter, there's a lot more going on than vengeance."

"Now, Dr. Brown, I watched the initial video footage and read your report immediately after your interview with the defendant. You had initially diagnosed him with psychosis. Why are you now claiming his diagnosis as bipolar?"

"Psychosis is more or less a sublevel to bipolar disorder. It's also in the same family as schizophrenia. I had originally diagnosed him with psychosis based on our interviews, but a proper diagnosis for psychosis includes blood testing, which came back a couple days later with no signs of psychosis."

"So you made an incorrect diagnosis at first?"

"I wouldn't call it incorrect, I simply didn't have all the information required to make it an official diagnosis. Once I read his blood tests, I changed the diagnosis to bipolar disorder."

"What's the difference, then, between the two disorders?"

"Psychosis is technically easier to diagnose, as there is concrete evidence in the bloodwork, whereas bipolar disorder relies more on a doctor's evaluation."

"So at the end of the day, your diagnosis is based more on your professional opinion rather than the hard science?"

"Well, no. I was able to eliminate psychosis *because* of the hard science."

"I see. Thank you, Dr. Brown, no further questions."

Murmuring spread from the back, and Jeremy felt a shift in the mood.

Linda stood and straightened her blazer with quick strokes of each hand. "Your Honor, the defense rests."

"Let's take a thirty-minute recess before closing statements." Judge Zamora banged the gavel, causing a flood of chatter.

32

Chapter 32

Monday, November 6, 2017

"Ladies and gentlemen of the jury, we're about to begin the process of closing statements," Judge Zamora said. "Please keep in mind that these statements are not factual evidence and are meant to be a summary of all the evidence presented. In no way should the following statements be used in your deliberation."

The judge took a sip from the cup of water on his bench. "Mr. Batchelor, you may begin."

"Thank you, Your Honor."

Just as he had begun his opening statements, Geoff stood in front of the jury box, pointing a remote at the television on the opposite wall.

The screen flickered to show a slideshow, scrolling through each of the thirteen victims in pictures. The courtroom fell silent as these pictures scrolled, before the screen cut to black and a muffled noise blared from the speakers.

"There's gunshots!" a crackled voice shrieked as the steady firing of a rifle echoed in the background. "There's blood everywhere! There's fucking bodies all over!"

The recorded 911 call cut out, and Geoff let the tension from the clip hang in the air before speaking.

"Those faces you just saw on the screen were thirteen innocent lives lost on March 11, 2016. The sound you heard was him." He stepped back and pointed directly at Jeremy, who kept his gaze facing forward, in the judge's direction.

"Those thirteen lives lost were mothers. Fathers. Sisters. Brothers. Friends. Grandchildren. Coworkers."

Geoff paused for effect.

"Everyone goes through a point in their professional career where things don't go their way. We get passed up for promotions. We get told one thing, and another thing happens. We get rejected for a raise after working so hard. We go through breakups, and gain and lose friends. This is normal. This is called life.

"What is not normal is to respond to these life events by bringing a semiautomatic weapon to the workplace and shooting every breathing person in sight. There's no place for that in our society. We are a humane race. Killing is wrong. Opening fire on defenseless, innocent people is downright despicable. Anyone who thinks otherwise deserves to be removed from society.

"Over the last couple weeks, you've heard a lot of graphic testimony. Your lives will be forever changed by being on this trial. You've seen images and heard things that cannot easily be erased from the mind. Every single person you saw take the witness stand will also be affected forever by what that man did.

"You've heard a lot about mental health, especially in the past few days of this trial. It's your due diligence to take mental health into consideration. I will never dismiss mental illness as a cause for bad actions; however, I also ask you to look at the big picture.

"That man over there felt as if the world were collapsing around him. In the months leading up to March 11, 2016, he lost a girlfriend in an ugly breakup, he was rejected not once, but twice for a promotion with his company. He had to work under a new manager who he felt was less qualified than himself. He was placed on probation by his company. He was turned down for a raise during his annual review, after having received generous raises every year prior.

"And while all this was happening, money started to disappear from his checking account. Cash was withdrawn. A semiautomatic rifle was purchased. Anger turned to rage. We'll never know for sure why the money was withdrawn. We didn't get to hear from the defendant directly. You are left to fill in those blanks.

"If something doesn't make sense, then it's probably not true. There are a lot of gaps in the story regarding his mental state of mind. There's been two different possible mental illnesses presented: one that would excuse his actions, and one that deems him legally sane at the time of the shootings. Legally sane means that he knew exactly what he was doing on March 11, and knew it was wrong.

"A firearm was purchased, along with hundreds of rounds of ammunition. He bought them ahead of time, suggesting that this disturbing thought had been brewing in his mind and was *not* a spur of the moment decision.

"The office's exit doors were barricaded with two-by-four pieces of wood. Every exit was locked except for the front doors that he entered through. This door was the furthest exit from the shooting, and I propose that he planned it this way on purpose. All of this points to some sort of planning. Were those two-by-fours just randomly convenient to him when he decided that morning he would shoot his coworkers in cold blood? I doubt it.

"You have thousands of pieces of evidence to go through. You have hard facts. Use these, along with your common sense, to decide what makes the most sense.

"Crimes of passion are done as a knee-jerk reaction. There's no calculation that goes into a crime of passion or rage. If he had gone to his car and come back in with his assault rifle right after he was rejected for a promotion or raise, then we'd be having a different conversation. But that's not what happened. This attack happened months after the rejected promotions, and weeks after the rejected raise. A travesty like this would have taken a long time to plan.

"When you deliberate, I want you to remember not only the lives lost, but also the thousands of lives affected by this horrific crime—a crime that was done with intent, and was calculated from beginning to end. Thank you."

The courtroom remained silent as Geoff returned to his seat. He sat back and crossed his arms. There were no more notes to take, no more cross-examinations to make. He was done and the case was in the jury's hands.

Jeremy stared across the aisle and wanted nothing more than to choke the blond motherfucker with his bare hands. The opening statements were tense, and Jeremy had been nervous at the time. Now, with the tension settled and having been in the same room with Geoff for more than two weeks straight, Jeremy felt no more nerves. He saw the justice system for the cat-and-mouse game it was, and the district attorney had played it as well as expected.

He didn't like the way he'd pointed that scrawny finger at him, and certainly didn't take kindly to the way he addressed him as *that man*. He might as well have called him *that monster in the cheap suit*.

But Jeremy also felt gratitude toward the D.A. He had just mentioned the thousands of lives affected by the shooting, and that *was* the point: affect lives, expose mental illness on the grandest stage possible, and change the world. Jeremy thought all the talk of schizotypal and bipolar disorders were utter bullshit. He had no mental illness. He didn't enjoy shooting his coworkers (except for Shelly), and had no desire to do something like that again. All he wanted was justice for those poor souls, forever trapped in their own minds, shunned by society when all they want is some goddamn help.

Linda stood, and Jeremy could feel her confidence radiate like heat waves as she approached the podium.

"Ladies and gentlemen of the jury, good afternoon." She stood five feet in front of the jury box and had their complete attention.

"This has been a draining and emotional trial. Probably the hardest one I've worked on in my long career. I'm just as disturbed as you all by the images and testimony we've seen. The actions committed by my client are nothing short of disgusting."

What the fuck is she doing?

"However, there's a major problem here. My client is suffering from bipolar disorder. He was suffering before the shooting, during the shooting, and still is to this day. He currently is on medication to treat this disorder.

"I will not stand here and say that my client didn't commit the crime. He did. He entered his office building with a semiautomatic firearm and shot thirty-five of his colleagues. However, that's not what this trial is about.

"My client has been suffering from a mental disorder that none of us can relate to. Not myself, not Mr. Batchelor, not any of yourselves, for you wouldn't be allowed to serve on a jury with such an illness.

"I want you to imagine having minimal control over your emotions. I want you to imagine having joy in life, then having it completely gone in a flash without knowing why. I want you to imagine your everyday struggles in life and how you would handle those without any sense of self-control.

"What do you normally do after a stressful day or week at work? Go home? Drink a beer and relax? Know that tomorrow is a new day and things can change?

"Mr. Heston used to do these things. He did them like you would. Then over time, like a cancer, this illness in his mind started to expand and slowly take full control.

"Mr. Heston was just like you. He liked to go out with his friends, celebrate with coworkers after a long week, go to sporting events with family. Slowly, the joy in those activities started to fade, and no one realized it. The life was sucked from him and those closest to him figured he was just settling into the typical grind of life.

"Unfortunately, that wasn't the case. In a time of dire need, Mr. Heston needed friends and family who simply weren't there. He felt that he was in the most frightening position in life: alone.

"Mental illness is real. It's not a ploy made up to try and get criminals an easy way out. It's very real—however, it's not palpable like a broken arm. If you break an arm, everyone sees your cast and wants to sign it. They want to ask what happened.

How long will you be in the cast?

"The problem with mental illness is that it cannot be seen. There's no cast, no story to tell, just insufferable pain from a broken mind. Jeremy Heston tried to battle this alone, as no one could see his injury. A broken mind that no longer had a place to run acted out in violence. A broken mind had exhausted its options, with nowhere to turn. A broken mind that could have been treated if there were only a way to visibly see it.

"Mr. Heston had lost touch with reality. He still suffers from a mental disease that has been developing for years. When he walked into that office, the evidence is clear that he could not control his thoughts. He could not control his actions. He could not control his perceptions.

"Mr. Batchelor brought up the notion of holes in the story. I hope you were paying attention to the holes in *his* story. The ultimate sign of sanity in a case like this is premeditation. Did Mr. Heston premeditate this attack? Did he do any sort of planning? There is not a shred of evidence that suggests so. The question you need to ask yourself is: could this have been done on the spur of the moment?

"Mr. Heston purchased the firearm months before the attack, during a time of peace in his life. He enjoyed the sport of shooting, something he had done many times with his uncle. Mr. Batchelor claims the ammunition couldn't have been purchased that morning, but nothing was ever proven about the time of purchase. There's no paper trail to show a transaction. Those rounds could have been purchased the same day as the firearm. The two-by-fours in his car could have come from anywhere. They could've been in his car for months. It's unfair and unjust to assume they were purchased with the intent of barricading his coworkers, without any proof of purchase. Your deliberation will be based on the facts, and there are no facts to support this claim of advance preparation.

"I ask all of you to be strong. The popular and easy verdict will be the guilty verdict, but please consider the big picture. A man is suffering from a serious mental illness and needs medical help. Acquitting him on the basis of his sanity will not be a popular decision, but that doesn't mean it will be the wrong decision. History is at stake here and you can be on the right side of it. Don't be afraid to go against the norm. Take mental health for the serious issue it truly is. Thank you."

Noses sniffled and Jeremy swore he could hear his mom crying, but refused to look over his shoulder. He had the urge to stand and applaud Linda. She'd done it. She gave it her all and now he was in as good a position as possible.

Now he remembered Linda's instructions to keep an eye on how the judge presented instructions to the jury. Even though judges had no say in the verdict, they still had an opinion, and the jury usually voted in the same manner as the judge. He could slant his instructions to favor one way or another.

"Thank you, Ms. Kennedy. Ladies and gentlemen of the jury, I will now instruct you on deliberations and how you should approach them," Judge Zamora said. "Earlier I instructed you on the law and how it applies to the court proceedings. When you return to the deliberation room, your first task will be to appoint a foreperson to preside over the deliberations. The foreperson has no special privilege, their vote counts the same as everyone else's; they are simply there to assure the deliberations are conducted in a quick and reasonable manner.

"As a reminder, you're still forbidden from discussing this case outside of the jury room. You are not allowed to use technology to retrieve additional information, and can only use all of the evidence, which will be provided to you.

"During your deliberations, you are allowed to take breaks as you see fit. However, be aware that the case cannot be discussed unless all twelve of you are present. Please make sure the clerk knows of your whereabouts should you choose to leave the jury room. The clerk will also take your cell phones when you are in the jury room. When you have reached a verdict and signed the verdict form, you will call us and we will then gather the parties back to the courtroom to announce your verdict.

"Until your verdict is announced in open court, no juror is permitted to disclose to anyone the status of your deliberations or the nature of your verdict.

"Circumstances in the case may arouse sympathy for one party or the other. Sympathy is a common, human emotion. The law does not expect you to be free of such normal reactions. However, the law, and your oath as jurors, require that you not permit sympathy to influence your verdict.

"It is your duty to weigh the evidence, decide the disputed questions of fact, apply the instructions of law to your findings, and render your unanimous verdict accordingly. Your duty as jurors is to arrive at a fair and just verdict.

"Consult with one another in the jury room, and deliberate with a plan of reaching an agreement. Each of you must decide the case for yourself. You should do so, however, only after a discussion of the case with the other jurors. Do not hesitate to change your opinion if convinced that it is wrong. However, you should not surrender your opinion in order to be congenial or solely to reach a verdict.

"Are there any questions?"

The jurors shook their heads.

"Very well. You are excused to the jury room to begin

deliberations for the final hour of the day."

Judge Zamora banged his gavel and Jeremy felt destiny wrap its unforgiving fingers around his soul. The trial was over and his fate now officially rested in the hands of the jury.

33

Chapter 33

Monday, November 6, 2017

Cathleen Speidel knew what she had to do. The man who had approached her in early October remained vivid in her mind, and she couldn't afford to take any chances.

She was the first to enter the deliberation room and she watched as the jurors settled in. The room had beige walls with a long, cherry-wood table at its center. White-cushioned swivel chairs awaited on each end, along with five others on each side of the table, to make a total of twelve. The only window in the room provided a stunning view of the Rocky Mountains, which had been hidden for most of the trial thanks to a nasty storm forming along the Front Range. Along the back wall was a lounge area, with a circle of four leather sofas, water and coffee machines, and a refrigerator stocked with snacks and lunch boxes brought by the jurors. A lone clock also hung on the wall, ticking away the seconds—the only means of telling time, since their phones had to be turned in before entering the deliberation room.

"I'll volunteer as foreman," Cathleen said from a middle seat when everyone took their places around the table. "Does anyone else have interest in doing it?"

The jurors looked around, shaking their heads.

"Sounds like it's all yours," a middle-age woman covered in jewelry said. "Be our guest."

"Okay, then," Cathleen said, grateful there was no objection. "Since we only have forty-five minutes left today, I think we should see where we are as a group so we can game plan for tomorrow. Let's each put down what we think the verdict should be on a piece of paper. Don't write your name on it, and put it in the center of the table when you're done. Remember that we have three choices: guilty, not guilty, or not guilty by reason of insanity."

Stay calm. This will be a process. Don't be pushy.

Everyone grabbed a pen from the table and scribbled on their notepads, ripping off the sheet of paper and folding it into a small square to toss in the middle of the table.

After a couple minutes, when everyone had finished, she pulled the pile of papers toward herself, unfolding each and flattening them on the table. She tallied each vote on her notepad as she opened it.

"Wow," she said as everyone watched in anticipation. "We're evenly split. Six guilty, six not guilty by reason of insanity."

She paused, her stomach churning. *This is gonna be an uphill battle.*

"Well, this is gonna be a long process," Aaron Elliott said. Aaron was one of the three men on the jury, dressed in a fine suit every day in court.

"Does anyone want to share their thoughts on where they stand?" Cathleen asked. "It's going to come out at some point, as we discuss the evidence and try to reach a unanimous verdict."

Two jurors said they voted not guilty while three others favored of a guilty verdict. No one elaborated as to why they felt one way or another, and it didn't spark the conversation Cathleen had hoped for.

"Does anyone else want to share right now?" Cathleen asked after a few seconds of silence. The remaining jurors who had not spoken remained silent.

A rapid knock came on the door and the deputy jury commissioner, Steve Linton, barged into the room with a line of suited people behind him. He had greeted the jurors every morning and kept their phones secured during the trial. He was a tall man, broad-shouldered, and had a permanent expression that showed he was not there to take shit from anyone. His military buzz cut and thick-framed glasses sparked an immediate intimidation. Behind the harsh facade was a gentle and friendly soul that Cathleen thought all the jurors had come to like over their weeks together.

Steve used both arms to cradle a large box, and the handful of people behind him carried similar boxes.

"I have evidence for you good folks," Steve said with a grin, dropping his box in front of Cathleen while the others placed theirs around the table. "There's more coming, too. Feel free to organize all the evidence as needed. Nothing is in any particular order, we just packed things as best we could. At this point, this is your evidence—do with it as you wish, just make sure to return everything to its corresponding evidence bag."

Steve and the others left the room and returned minutes later with another round of boxes.

The AR-15 used by Jeremy to commit the shooting stuck out of one of the boxes, shining under the lights, and they all stared at it in silence. A splatter of blood covered the barrel of the rifle.

"That's a big gun," one of the young women said. She had not yet offered her current opinion on the verdict.

"This should be everything," Steve said. "You have about fifteen minutes left today. The room will be locked once you all leave. Come find me if you have any questions."

"Thanks, Steve," Cathleen said as she pulled a box toward herself. "Alright all, we have the evidence. Do we want to go through each piece together and discuss? Or do more of a free-for-all?"

"Let's start with a free-for-all," the older man with the beard said. "Then we can discuss pieces of evidence that we feel are relevant. No need to go over every single bullet casing and whatnot."

"Sounds good to me," Cathleen said. "Let's start sifting through the boxes, and if you come across something to discuss, set it aside for the morning when we get back."

The jurors dove into the boxes, quiet chatter breaking out among them for the first time in a while. Their final minutes of the day passed and they all left the courthouse with a new sense of energy. They had done the sitting, listening, and waiting over the last two weeks, and now it was their time to shine.

34

Chapter 34

Wednesday, November 8, 2017

Day 13 of the trial

Jeremy sat in his cell, elbows propped on his knees, his head resting on clasped hands. He'd spoken to God a lot more in recent days, when the realization had finally sunk in that none of this was in his hands.

After all his damned planning, perfecting, and execution—none of it mattered. He was a mass murderer, a monster who would surely be shot dead in the street if he was ever released. He was wasting taxpayers' time and money with his bullshit trial that would inevitably end with him locked up for life at the very least.

Why did I think I was special? What kind of fucked-up delusion did I have to think I could actually pull this off? Those jurors don't give a shit about my life—they want me dead like the rest of the world.

Dr. Siva came into his mind, and he remembered all of their late-night meetings, when they discussed life, politics, and work.

"You planted this idea in my head," Jeremy whispered. A

buzzing sound preceded the lights turning off. It was ten at night, time for bed. Time to ponder where it all went wrong. Wasn't that the point of jail?

If I never went through with all this, where would I be today?

He would've been fired on March 11, 2016. A single, unemployed life would have awaited him, but he could've bounced back. The last time he'd been fired from a job, a new company came calling to start the next chapter of his life. Now he could only wonder what that next chapter would have been.

Have you ever wondered if maybe those doctors are right? an inner voice asked. *Two doctors did diagnose you with a mental illness.*

"I'm not mentally ill. Absolutely not. I think I'd know if I was." Jeremy whispered to himself and stood up from his bed, pacing around his cell. He had never taken the thought seriously, so focused on selling himself as mentally ill. "Does a mentally ill person know that they're mentally ill?"

Of course not. Their lives continue as normal in their mind. They don't realize they're different until they end up in a situation like this.

"I'm not crazy. I'm not bipolar. I've been in charge the whole time." Jeremy shook the thought free, convinced everything had so far gone according to his plan.

Now there's only three possibilities: I live in the nut house until I die, I live in prison until I die, or I get sentenced to die.

Jeremy felt he had finally snapped out of the trance that had taken hold of him since late 2015, and his body trembled. The reality of the situation blanketed his emotions, turning him numb to the rest of the world. With three possible outcomes that all ended in death, all Jeremy wanted was to lie down and die.

I don't even have a plan in case I do get sent to the loony bin. What the fuck did I think would happen? I outsmart some psychiatrists and get released back into society? I'll never be allowed to see the world again, and if I somehow did, someone would find me and wipe me off the map themselves.

He couldn't even kill himself. The jail cells didn't allow for it. He could bash his head into the concrete walls, but he knew that would only knock him unconscious before he could land a final blow to cut out the lights for good. He had remained in solitary confinement the entire time, so he couldn't even bait some meathead into a fight to bash his brains in for him.

So I sit here to rot. Whatever happens in that courtroom, it all ends the same for me. I'm never going to have friends, never going to any more sports games with Uncle Ricky and my dad, I'm never going to love again, never going to see the world. It's just a long crawl to the finish line.

Jeremy started crying. The joke was on him. Society didn't give a shit about mental illness. If you kill innocent people, you get sentenced to life in prison or death; there's simply no tolerance for such actions in a healthy world.

"Snap out of it, Jeremy." He smacked himself on the head, snot dripping from his nose. "It's not over. Nothing's been decided yet."

What would I do if I got sent to the loony bin?

Having something to focus his mind on helped distract him from the doom that awaited.

Let's assume I get the insanity verdict. I'll be processed into a mental institution, but I'm not insane. I can find a way out. There's always a way out. I would be hunted if I escaped and would need to find a solid hiding spot, possibly move states after the initial hype dies down and live under a new alias. I could write a book about why I did it all and it could be the ultimate liberation for the mentally ill. I could—

"What the fuck?" Jeremy jumped. Through the darkness of the jail cell, he could make out the silhouette of a tall man standing at the cell door. The man stood stiffly, with his hands crossed in front of him. The body remained still and Jeremy could feel the man's eyes locked on his every movement. "Who are you?" Jeremy's voice trembled.

"Who I am doesn't matter." The voice came out of the darkness in a chilling, dark tone.

"What do you want from me?" Jeremy's heart drummed against his ribcage, and deep down he liked the adrenaline. He felt alive again.

"It's not what I want from you. It's what you know you want from yourself. You're a killer, Jeremy. Get back out there and kill, it's the only way."

"The only way to what?" Jeremy asked, seated at the edge of his bed, fists clenched.

"The only way to prove your grand scheme. The big experiment. You know, the reason you're here."

The body hadn't moved, as far as Jeremy could tell. Chills broke out down his spine.

"I killed to prove a point."

"You killed because you're crazy. People go through the same things you went through every day, and no one else shoots everyone around them. You see the world differently. You're special. Few people can slaughter others and claim it was in the name of science, to separate themselves from the guilt."

"I've felt plenty of guilt. I didn't want to kill any of those people."

"Precisely. You *had* to, right?"

197

Jeremy paused. Whoever the fuck this guy was, he knew exactly how to push his buttons. He felt the rage from several months ago start to boil up again.

"Who are you?" Jeremy kept his voice calm, despite having the urge to scream.

"First off," the man said, disregarding Jeremy's question, "I can feel that hot anger you have. I was worried it left you, but it's still there. You have a beast inside you that needs to be fed; stop trying to keep it trapped. Second, you don't know me, but you've seen me before."

Jeremy tried to focus on the dark voice, but couldn't recognize it for the life of him. *Who the fuck is this?*

"You saw me the morning of the shooting. You passed me in the doorway right when you entered the building."

Jeremy went back to that fateful day. Then he remembered.

"The man in the suit?" he asked.

"So you do remember me? Thought you would." Jeremy could hear a smile in the man's voice.

"I do remember, I almost shot you because I didn't know who you were. Why are you here? Who are you?"

"Well, Jeremy, why do you suppose I'm here?"

Jeremy's mind raced. How could this man have passed through all the security to visit him in his solitary cell?

"Are you real, or are you in my head?" Jeremy asked, his voice now wavering.

"I'm as real as you'd like. You bumped into me that morning, did you not?"

"Yeah?"

"And here I am, standing right in front of you. So you tell me, am I real?"

Jeremy's breathing picked up until it was near hyperventilation. *Am I fucking crazy? Am I seeing people?*

"You're made up. You're not real."

"Ah, I'm your imaginary friend? What an honor. I suppose I've been called worse, but for the most part when people see me they usually resist at first, then finally give in and leap for me. Another reason you're special: you've no urge to do such a thing despite the thoughts you had in here earlier tonight."

Jeremy closed his eyes and tried to imagine the man away. *He's not real. You're just having cabin fever and are seeing things. There really was a man in a suit that day at the office, and he's just a leftover in your subconscious.*

"Jeremy, you're going to do special things in the future. Keep your eye on the prize. Thirteen deaths is okay, but those are rookie numbers. I know you can do a lot better next time. Think it over, you'll find your way."

Then the figure stepped out of sight. Jeremy jumped off his bed and ran to the bars, grasping one in each head as he pressed his face into the space between them, craning for a look in the direction the man had gone.

A soft glow of light from a dormant computer screen was all he could see. No man, no suit. Nothing.

Jeremy laid back down, after smashing his face between the cell bars and frantically looking left and right. He couldn't remember what he'd been thinking about before the suited man showed up.

He took himself back to that day outside the office. The man with the black-slicked hair had winked at him when they passed each other in the doorway at Open Hands. Jeremy's duffel bag, slung over his shoulder, had brushed against the man's leg. That man was the last person he saw before he entered the office floor and turned it into a massacre.

Jeremy resisted sleep that night. He stared into the darkness of the ceiling, his mind unable to let go of that pale-skinned man. He played the wink over and over again until he eventually fell into a deep sleep.

35

Chapter 35

A whole week of deliberations passed. After the first two days passed without him being called back to the courthouse, Jeremy started to think he just might be getting off on the insanity plea. The small glimmer of hope completely flipped his confidence.

He still had an insane persona to maintain, and did so during the day when the cops were present. Even though the trial was technically over, he didn't want word to slip that he was acting normal. For twenty months he had maintained his insane personality by remaining silent and acting in a daze. When the medication treatment began, it was much easier to fall into an actual daze. But when the lights went out at night, Jeremy danced in his cell, overtaken by bursts of energy that had built up all day.

They can't take music from you. Music lives in the mind. While he couldn't remember every lyric to many of his favorite songs, he knew the beats, and that was enough for him to dance across the floor in a graceful motion he hadn't felt in years. If he planned to escape from a mental institution, he'd need to be in shape, so he started doing push-ups and crunches after his nightly dance sessions. It became a ritual for him to go to bed each night in a sweat-soaked uniform. The dampness, while not comfortable, gave him a sense of accomplishment.

His positivity snowballed with every hour that passed without a verdict being turned in. The visiting man felt like a distant memory. Of course Jeremy wouldn't kill again, that wasn't the point of all this. Still, he'd never forget the feeling of power when the bullets sprayed mercilessly across the office. All those terrified faces staring at him, all those screams pleading in the final moments of their lives.

It did feel good, he reminisced. *Just focus on getting out of here. Stay in shape, and be ready for what comes next. People escape prison all the time, it's not impossible. It could be a clerical error that sets you free. Just stay ready.*

Jeremy had a meeting planned with Linda later that morning. She wanted to fill him in on the legal process, what to expect moving forward, and her thoughts on the long deliberation. He spent his morning eating his favorite meal during his time in jail, a bland bowl of oatmeal with sliced banana on top and a short glass of milk to wash it all down.

When the officer came to take him to the visitor's room, Jeremy had fallen asleep for a late-morning nap, and was barked at to get the fuck out of bed.

When Jeremy arrived to the visitation room, Linda greeted him in her usual dress pants and blazer. "Good morning, Jeremy."

"Hello." *Back to being insane, stick to the plan.*

"How have you been the last week? Feels like forever since we've seen each other."

"I'm good. Just eating and sleeping."

"That's good. I wanted to have a quick meeting with you today and fill you in on some things."

"Okay."

"I expect a verdict to be turned in before the weekend. If not, it will happen on Monday for sure, but I highly doubt the jurors want to drag this out over another weekend."

"What will they say?"

Linda kept a serious face, but Jeremy could tell she was fighting off a grin. "Honestly, I have no idea, and that's a good thing. Going in, I believed there were two possibilities for deliberations: a quick one figured out within a day, where the verdict comes back guilty; or one that would take maybe three days or so and still come back guilty. I won't lie to you, this case was supposed to be near impossible to win. But here we are a week later, five full days of deliberation, and word is they still need some more time. That tells me they are having serious talks about your mental state and likely having debates on which way to go. That's as good of a chance as we could hope for."

Jeremy fought off a grin of his own. "I see," he said.

"Remember, should you be found guilty, then we continue in the courtroom to the sentencing phase, where you would either be sentenced to life in prison or the death penalty. This phase could take just as long, since the death penalty requires a unanimous decision. All it takes is one person to be opposed and you would avoid death."

Life in prison is still death, might even be worse.

"And if they find you innocent under the insanity plea, you would stay in this jail for another week or two while the court and mental hospital process loads of paperwork. The court will also decide the terms for your potential release from the hospital. They'll be near-impossible to meet, but they will be put in place."

Jeremy nodded.

"I'm still doing prep work, in case we go to the sentencing phase. Do you have any questions?"

Jeremy shook his head.

"Then I'll plan on seeing you later this week," she said.

He thanked her and she stood and stepped away, motioning to the guard to come and take Jeremy back to his cell.

Jeremy went back to his cell, wanting to dance and celebrate. Instead he had to settle for pacing in circles until his lunch arrived a few minutes later.

I'm not going to prison. I can feel it. Fuck the system. I just might pull this whole thing off.

36

Chapter 36

Friday, November 17, 2017
  Day 20 of the trial

Jeremy only knew the day of the week because of his meeting with Linda on Wednesday. When he had no appointments, the days were irrelevant. When he woke up Friday morning, he felt a stillness in the air that made him uneasy. The sounds of other inmates down the hall usually carried into his cell, but the jail was dead silent today. Daylight glowed from the hallway, and Jeremy figured the others had been granted outdoor time after the past week had been gloomy and snowy.

He sat up and saw his breakfast tray waiting for him on the ground: a bowl of plain cereal with an apple on the side. A fly buzzed around the apple, dipping down for a quick bite every couple seconds.

Jeremy stood from his cot and swayed on his feet as he did every morning. His thighs burned from the newly incorporated lunges he'd worked into his late-night exercise routine. Aside from that, he felt strong. He had never worked out regularly before coming to jail, but the free time allowed him to and the results were amazing as far as he was concerned. His once-flabby gut was now solid and his biceps started to bulge even when he was relaxed. He'd never been in a fistfight, but felt he could kick some ass if need be.

The guards didn't seem to notice or care. His jumpsuit was baggy and hid his progress. As far as they knew, he was a psychopath who stared at the wall all day.

He ate his cereal, his fly friend keeping him company, when a guard approached the barred door.

"Heston!" he barked. "You're due in court this afternoon. Your verdict is in."

Jeremy dropped his spoon into the nearly empty bowl and his hands immediately started to tremble.

"We'll be taking you over in two hours." The guard walked off, not interested in a response.

Holy fuck. Today's the day.

Jeremy remembered the feeling he'd had in the days leading up to the shooting. The anticipation became unbearable that final week, as he could sense his world was about to change. Now that tickle of destiny crept back up. He had adjusted to life in jail, not liking it by any means, but able to accept it was his life for the near future. Now it would all change again. Death row or a mental institution would flip his life from what he had grown accustomed to.

The cereal would remain unfinished, the apple only half eaten. His stomach was too tense to consider pushing anything else into it. He already felt as if he might vomit, and considered forcing himself to before leaving for the courthouse. The fact that his own attorney couldn't give a concrete prediction terrified and comforted him at the same time.

Over his first few months in jail, Jeremy had felt nothing but regret. Not for his actions, but for not having prepared beyond the actual day of the shooting. He had done research on the legality of his planned crime, but put no energy into how the public would react.

All mass shootings followed a similar course. The week following a shooting was filled with useless thoughts and prayers for the victims, then everyone went back to life as normal. For whatever reason, society was shackled by the misconception that there was no way to change the ever-growing gun obsession.

Fortunately, Jeremy wasn't out to policy change the untouchable Second Amendment, but rather to influence society's views on mental illness. The trial revolved around his supposed mental illness, and if he ended up getting a good verdict later today, it might cause the slightest shift in how people viewed mental health. Or they would be outraged and riot in the streets.

* * *

The drive from the jail to the courthouse felt longer than normal. There were only two stoplights, and they caught both of them red. Jeremy's stomach felt like a wet cloth being wrung out to dry, but he managed to keep his hands from trembling. The officer didn't speak a word as usual and ignored the messages coming across his radio.

When they arrived at the courthouse parking lot, a mob of reporters waited at the back entrance, where they knew Jeremy would be escorted. There had been handfuls before, at various times throughout the trial, but a quick glance suggested at least fifty members of the press waiting, flashing cameras as the car came to a stop directly in front of the door.

The officer opened the door for Jeremy, placed a hand on his arm, and guided him toward the entrance as the press shouted at him.

"Jeremy, what do you think will happen?" asked one.

"Are you prepared for a guilty verdict?" asked another.

"How are you coping with all of the world watching you?" shouted another.

All of the world? It occurred to him that he had no idea how wide of a reach this trial had. Sure there were cameras in the courtroom, but he figured a majority of the TV audience would be Colorado locals and a few people around the country who knew someone affected in the shooting. But the whole world? That reporter had to have been exaggerating.

As instructed by Linda early on, Jeremy remained silent as he entered the courthouse and heard the shouting of reporters reduced to a murmur behind the closed door. The officer guided him to his special holding room.

"Should be about a half hour before you're due in court. I'll be back for you then." The officer vanished and left Jeremy to spin in his racing mind.

Okay. It's okay. This is what this has all been for.

He felt a sudden urge to shit, but had to fight it off as that opportunity wouldn't come until after the verdict. It was just bubble guts anyway—he had to focus on calming himself down. His suit was laid across the table, and as he changed, he wondered if he'd ever have to put on the dark red jumpsuit again.

The thirty minutes felt more like two hours as Jeremy waited in the isolated room. He loved the room as it had a window, and he stared out at the snow-capped mountains in the distance, remembering the shooting sessions he'd had at his Uncle Ricky's cabin many moons ago.

The door swung open to bring him back to present time. "Let's go," the officer said coldly. Jeremy stood and his legs felt like gelatin, wobbly and unstable.

He took slow steps across the room before the officer grabbed his arm and pulled him toward the door to enter the courtroom. The world came to a brief standstill as Jeremy stood before the door, every defining moment of his life flashing into his mind in quick snippets. His childhood, his parents, starting school, friends, teachers, graduation, falling in love. Jamie. It was funny how fast life could go by, and yet those special memories remain frozen in time like portraits on a wall.

The door opened to the courtroom, and all eyes in the gallery immediately shifted to him. They were just as eager as he was to know the outcome. He saw his parents in the front row behind Linda and refused eye contact once again. Locking eyes with either of them would melt his soul into a puddle of tears, especially if the verdict came back guilty.

Jeremy blacked out for a moment, not conscious of walking across the courtroom and taking his seat next to Linda before the bailiff shouted, "All rise!"

Jeremy stood along with the rest of the room as Judge Zamora entered from his chambers.

"Good afternoon, folks, please be seated," the judge said calmly. "Does counsel have any matters to discuss before we get started?"

Geoff and Linda shook their heads.

"Okay. The verdict has been submitted by the jury. I'll read the verdict first—I've not seen it yet—and then will briefly ensure some clerical matters are in place before announcing it.

"I want to address everyone in the courtroom first. Regardless of the outcome of this verdict, I need you to remain silent as I read through this information. Keep in mind, there are dozens of counts against the defendant, and a verdict will be given to each count. If you feel you can't contain your emotions, please exit the courtroom quietly.

"Now let's bring in the jury." Judge Zamora gestured to the door they would enter from and the bailiff crossed the room to open it.

The jurors took their usual slow stride into the jury box, stone-faced. When the final juror sat, Judge Zamora turned to address them.

"Ladies and gentlemen of the jury, I want to thank you for your service during this long and emotional trial. Your time and dedication are deeply appreciated by the state and county. Is your verdict ready for me to review?"

Ms. Serious stood from her position in the first seat, closest to the judge. "Yes, Your Honor."

"And you have reached a unanimous decision as a group and have submitted that verdict to Mr. Linton?"

"Yes, Your Honor."

"Very well, thank you for following procedure. Ms. Matthis, do you have the verdict forms ready?" he asked the courtroom clerk seated in front of the bench.

"Yes, Your Honor." She stood with a manila envelope in her grip.

My fate is in that envelope. The world slowed as Jeremy watched Judge Zamora pull a small stack of papers out of the envelope. His mind and body froze, unable to bear the intensity of the situation.

The judge flipped through the stack of papers, running a finger down each page until he found the bit of information he needed.

Each turn of the page dragged in slow motion before the judge spoke directly to Jeremy.

"Will the defendant please stand for the reading of the verdict?"

Jeremy rose, the eyes of the world glued to him.

"Mr. Heston, as a reminder I will read one of three possible verdicts for each of the charges brought against you: guilty, not guilty, or not guilty by reason of insanity. Now let's begin."

Judge Zamora hesitated as he organized the stack of verdicts. The silence hung in the room as Jeremy's arms started to tremble. The judge cleared his throat before unleashing Jeremy's destiny.

"For the first count of murder in the first degree of Shelly Williams, the jury finds the defendant not guilty by reason of insanity."

Gasps echoed across the courtroom, and someone shrieked. Jeremy could hear every single sound in the room, and the gasp made his heart race as he realized what the judge had just said.

"For the second count of murder in the first degree of Mark Fernandez, the jury finds the defendant not guilty by reason of insanity."

More murmurs in the crowd, along with people sighing and groaning in disgust.

"For the third count of murder in the first degree of Sylvia Jones, the jury finds the defendant not guilty by reason of insanity."

Sylvia.

She didn't die in vain after all. Jeremy would finally get to proceed with his experiment and make sure the lives lost were an integral part of changing the world. He had seen Sylvia's son sitting in the audience and wanted nothing more than to apologize for taking such a great mother away from him. He wished he could make him understand that there was a silent killer spreading across the country—mental illness—which could now be stopped.

The judge continued reading down the list of charges for first-degree murder, followed by the not guilty by reason of insanity verdict. Each name weighed down on Jeremy, hearing them listed for what would hopefully be the final time. He could hear a couple of people in the audience sobbing.

Each count and verdict that Judge Zamora read helped the reality settle in for Jeremy. He was not getting lethal injection; he was not spending the rest of his life in prison. He was going to a mental institution, where doctors with more knowledge than he had would try to treat his fake mental illness.

I actually did it. I'm going to change the world.

Chapter 37

Friday, November 17, 2017

Outside the courthouse, Connor Chappell walked to his car, tears pouring down his face. His brother, Charlie, had been killed in the Open Hands office shooting, but apparently no one on the jury gave a shit about his life or any of the other lives taken that day. They sympathized with the monster and his bullshit mental illness.

Connor had watched that monster every day on TV during the trial. He watched his brother's killer sit through all the graphic testimony, never showing a single sign of remorse—yet now he would avoid jail time and be coddled at a mental hospital, and then one day set free.

Connor wished he knew which cars in the lot belonged to the jurors, because he would have loved to bash in their windows and set them on fire.

"Fuck!" he yelled, and it echoed back to him in the empty parking lot. Everyone was still in the courtroom, as the judge wrapped up the final instructions and next steps. He couldn't sit in that room anymore; he wanted to get as far from it as possible. Media vans lined up at the front of the courthouse, mobs of press fighting their way inside for a chance to interview survivors and family members of the deceased.

They were lucky he was able to slip out unnoticed. He would have told them to take their stupid questions and shove them up their asses.

He arrived at his car too angry to drive, body shaking in rage. He pictured his brother lying lifeless on the office floor, blood oozing out of the bullet wound on his forehead. His brother had a bright future ahead, with a beautiful fiancée. Now none of it would happen.

"But Jeremy *fucking* Heston gets to live the rest of his shitty life."

Connor kicked the driver-side door, and punched the hood, then screamed in pain, echoing across the parking lot.

"Don't worry, Charlie," he said, climbing into the driver's seat, his knuckles already swelling. "You're not going out like this. I'm gonna kill that piece of shit if it's the last thing I do."

* * *

Inside the courtroom, the people in the gallery erupted after the verdict reading was complete, causing Judge Zamora to furiously bang his gavel. Some shouted in the direction of Jeremy and his parents, others broke down into tears, defeated by the verdict. Jeremy could *feel* the looks of disgust being thrown his way as he remained standing. His parents sat in the front row as they had the entire trial, and he turned his head just enough to see his mom out of the corner of his eye. He saw her shoulders convulsing as she hid her face behind her hands, his father's arm slung over her shoulders.

I'm sorry, Mom and Dad. This trial must have been overwhelming.

At this moment all he could do was wish the judge would finish with his business. He wanted to be alone so he could celebrate in private.

It worked. My plan actually worked. I'm going to a mental institute where I can continue my work! Jeremy felt the urge to scream, cry, and laugh all at the same time. He fought to keep the bomb of emotions from exploding, even though it wouldn't have mattered at this point.

Judge Zamora finally fell silent, stacking the verdict papers into a neat pile. Jeremy caught Ms. Serious looking at him; she turned her face when he briefly locked eyes with her.

"Mr. Heston, you may be seated," Judge Zamora said.

Linda stared at the judge, and Jeremy could see the slightest smirk at the corner of her mouth. Her career had just changed forever; she had done the impossible.

"Mr. Heston, a jury of your peers has found you not guilty by reason of insanity. You'll be moved to the Rocky Mountain Mental Health Institute in Pueblo, Colorado. You'll remain there and undergo mental health examinations until a panel of their staff can unanimously agree that you're no longer a threat to yourself or society.

"You will be taken there next week. Until then, you'll remain in custody. I'll enforce extra security for the remainder of the week and during the transfer to Pueblo, at which point you'll be in the hands of the hospital."

The judge turned his attention to the jury and informed them they could now speak of the trial, including to the press waiting outside the courthouse. He also offered the jurors the chance to wait back in their room while the crowd outside died down. They would have security to guide them to their cars.

Jeremy leaned forward to see the district attorney across the aisle. His pale face now looked ghostlike. Jeremy savored seeing the shame spreading through the blond prick's body.

"And that concludes this trial. Thank you to everyone for your hard work. Court is adjourned."

At the final bang of the gavel the crowd burst out, crying and yelling.

"You'll get your justice in hell!" someone shouted. The bailiff pushed his way into the mob of people and escorted a middle-age woman out of the courtroom. Jeremy saw none of this as he stared forward. He wanted to see his parents, but there was no way he was going to turn around and face all the hate he could feel behind him.

"We did it," Linda said, patting Jeremy on the arm. Her smirk had grown into a full-on smile.

"You did it," Jeremy said. "I just sat here."

Linda nodded, accepting the compliment.

"So what now?" Jeremy asked. "Do we say good-bye?"

"Yes. Our work here is done. I'll be checking in with you from time to time at the hospital. I'll make sure you're being treated right. I assume your parents will also come see you there."

"How long until you think I have a chance of getting released from the hospital?"

Linda paused and frowned. "It will be a very long time, if ever. The soonest they'll probably consider it is maybe twenty-five years from now. At that point...it's hard to say. You'll always be deemed a threat to society."

"Doesn't sound much different from prison."

"It's very different from prison. You'll probably start in some sort of solitary confinement, but as long as you show them that you're no longer violent, you'll be able to mix in with the other patients in no time. On top of that, you'll have much better food, free time to do whatever you want on campus, and of course, outdoors time."

Linda made it sound like he was going to a five-star resort instead of the nuthouse.

"I think it's time for you to head back," she said as Jeremy's escorting officer approached them.

"Thanks again," Jeremy said. "I don't know how I can ever repay you."

Linda shook her head. "It was my pleasure. I hope you get the treatment you need."

Her words sounded fake and forced. He wouldn't be surprised if she was disgusted with herself for getting him off on insanity. But she had a job to do, and her future now had every possibility open to her, thanks to the unlikely victory.

"Bye, Linda."

* * *

Through the initial planning of his experiment, it had felt like he'd never get to this point. Now the hardest part was over. The world would be forever changed by his verdict. A mass murderer was actually walking "free" by avoiding prison. Jeremy could feel the mental health community collectively, and silently, rejoicing in his victory. Instead of being a footnote in a long history of gun violence, his name would show as the ever important turning point in American society where mentally ill people received fair treatment from the justice system. He fought the odds, blasted through the glass ceiling of the court system, and felt he had just reached the top of Mount Everest.

Now what? he wondered.

He had planned and pulled off a meticulous mass shooting, with the precise goal of being caught and getting off on the insanity plea. He had wanted to shed light on the mental health epidemic, which seemed to be constantly swept under the rug by society.

Now that he'd done it—now what?

He hoped he would be able to write in a notebook at the Rocky Mountain Mental Health Institute. *Will my writings be monitored?* His doodles in a notebook would only further confirm his "insanity." But his ultimate plan was to expose to the world what happened in the hospital, along with his journey there, in a sort of memoir.

Jeremy was led out of the courtroom, toward the back of the police car to drive him back to jail for the final time. The angry crowd had forced their way to the back exit of the courthouse where they gathered to greet the "innocent" murderer.

"Rot in hell!" a sobbing mother shouted.

"I'll kill you myself if we ever meet!" shouted a voice from the back.

A handful of officers created a perimeter around Jeremy's path to the squad car. The shouting people fed off each other, elevating the noise into a blur. *There's gotta be fifty people back here*, Jeremy thought.

"Motherfucker!" a woman screamed from the front of the group. She resembled Janae, and he wondered if she was her mother.

Look at the uproar I'm already causing. Jeremy kept his stare on the squad car as he maneuvered toward it.

Then he decided to have some fun with his new fans.

Before he sat down in the car, he looked back at the crowd and grinned as widely and maniacally as he could. The crowd roared, throwing fists in the air, screaming in a chaotic symphony.

The squad car pulled away as the sun broke through the clouds for the first time all week.

38

Chapter 38

Thursday, November 23, 2017

The weekend following the verdict ended up different than any of Jeremy's previous days in jail. He was stripped of his dark red jumpsuit that was saved for the most dangerous of inmates, his shackles were removed, and he was granted outdoor time, an hour each day.

He was still required to remain in solitary, even during his outdoor time, as there was legitimate concern for his safety among the other inmates. Infamous inmates were always a target. The threats weren't as likely in a county jail as they might be at a maximum security prison, but they were present nonetheless.

The officers couldn't care less about his not-guilty verdict, and would continue to be short with him, barking orders in his ear and "accidentally" bumping into him.

Jeremy didn't know how much control they had over the water pressure, but his final shower in jail felt like an air attack from a nail gun. It shot out of the showerhead in a burning stream; they had to have turned up the heat. Red marks showed across Jeremy's back as he took his final, naked walk of shame around the shower room to where an officer waited with towels.

Jeremy put all the harshness and cruelty behind him. He knew the officers were pissed with the verdict. Some of them were first responders—or friends with first responders—who had their lives forever scarred by his actions.

"It was worse than the shit I saw in Iraq," Jeremy heard one officer tell another the week after the shooting.

"How could one person cause all that damage?" asked another.

Police officers understood the dangers of their jobs, but they never expected to see a scene like they saw on March 11, 2016.

After the weekend passed, Jeremy spent his final days in jail plotting his next move. Linda had stopped by to inform him of the next steps.

"You're going to be transferred to Pueblo on Thursday." It was Monday morning when she came to see him, leaving him with three more days in jail. "When you arrive at the institute, you'll be processed into a solitary room. You need to understand that, at first, you'll be in a straightjacket and a padded room."

"What? Why?"

"It's procedure. Since you received the insanity verdict, you'll be treated as a new insanity patient by the hospital. I've sent over paperwork vouching for your good behavior in jail over the last year, so I suspect you'll only spend a couple days with this arrangement. You'll also meet your doctor, Dr. Harriet Carpenter. Dr. Carpenter works for the hospital and will be visiting with you at least five days each week. She has been in this line of work for a very long time and will be focused on getting your mind back to a healthy state."

Now's the time to tell her. Everything from this point forward needs to be focused on getting me out of the mental hospital.

"Linda, I need to tell you something and I hope you can hear me out. This was all a big plan. I'm not mentally ill. I'm normal. I've made very detailed plans to get to this point. I'm trying to expose mental health to the public. I'm going to write a book about my experience in the mental hospital. *Insane Like Me* is going to be the title."

Linda stared at him blankly. He had spoken in the most formal voice he could muster, the one he used when he needed to bullshit Shelly back in the day.

"Okay, Jeremy, if you say so. Dr. Carpenter will be helping you, you should maybe take this up with her."

She doesn't believe me! I've been holding this in for more than a year, and now that I tell her she doesn't fucking believe me!

"Linda, I'm not kidding. I planned all of this out in a notebook."

"Jeremy, I don't have time for this. You've been diagnosed and are going to get treatment."

"I'm not lying!" Jeremy slammed his fist on the table.

Linda jumped back in her chair, but didn't stand. "Jeremy, why should I believe this? I've been working on your case for the past year—all of my energy on your insanity defense. We found a doctor who diagnosed you with a serious mental condition, and now you're trying to tell me it's all a lie? Pardon my French, but that is pure bullshit."

"I swear to you."

"Where is this supposed notebook?" Linda's face turned to stone as she peered at Jeremy.

"I threw it away at a gas station in Golden."

"Well, that's convenient."

"It's the truth. Why don't you believe me?"

"Jeremy, you need serious help. You're delusional. Have you stopped taking your pills?"

"No!" Jeremy snapped, baffled that she refused to believe the truth. *The pills may have started losing their effect, but what difference does it make?*

"Why don't you believe me?" His hands started to shake, and she noticed.

"Okay, let's pretend for a second that I believe this story of yours. Why are you telling me now? And what exactly do you want me to do with this information? You've already received a not-guilty verdict."

"It will get me out of the hospital faster. My mind is healthy and perfectly fine."

"Jeremy, you're not okay. This might all seem normal in your mind, but it's not. You are insane. Period. For Christ's sake, the prosecution's psychiatrist called you insane, and it was his job to prove otherwise! I'll be sharing this information alright—with Dr. Carpenter. All you're doing is further proving your mental instability. I'm leaving now. Good luck, Jeremy."

Linda hung up her phone and walked out of the room.

* * *

When Thursday morning arrived, Jeremy jumped out of bed at sunrise. He'd been waking up energetically for the past few weeks thanks to his late-night workout routine, but the upcoming change had kept him in a light sleep Wednesday night.

Today he would finally leave jail. He couldn't believe he had managed to execute his plan, despite Linda refusing to believe it.

"Good morning," Jeremy said to his empty cell. A good morning it was, as he received his favorite breakfast and ate it in peace.

What will the food be like in the loony bin?

He wondered this, along with many other things, about his new home.

The officer on duty informed Jeremy that he would be leaving at ten and his processing would begin at nine sharp. The guards' resentment was still palpable from the dirty looks and irritated tones they spoke with.

The two officers who arrived at nine to escort him didn't speak a word. They were two towering men with crossed arms and stern expressions. Jeremy stood from his bed and approached the door with his hands extended to be handcuffed.

The officer with a thick mustache slapped on the cuffs with more force than necessary, while the other unlocked the door and slid it open. Jeremy felt a fluttering within himself. He was soon to be a "free" man.

He was led to a back room, where another officer stood behind a tall desk, clicking and typing on his computer.

"Heston?" he asked as they all entered.

Like you don't know who I am.

Jeremy grinned at the officer. "Yes, sir."

"Have a seat while I pull up your file."

The officer—Clanton, according to his badge—gestured to the seats across the small room and kept his head down as he typed on the computer. Jeremy's escorting officers stood in the doorway and waited in awkward silence.

I can't believe I'm actually leaving this shithole.

Ten minutes passed before Officer Clanton spoke again.

"Heston. I have your things."

He pulled a plastic bag from behind the desk and plopped it on top.

What things?

Clanton pulled out clothing from the bag and Jeremy's blood chilled to ice as he saw the black hoodie he was wearing on the day of the shooting. He approached the desk.

"I have one black hooded sweater, one T-shirt, one pair of jeans, one wallet with $26, two credit cards, and a driver's license, one pair of tennis shoes, and one cell phone."

Jeremy never thought he would see these things again—but he was being treated like any other prisoner and given back what he had entered with twenty months earlier. He remembered the shoes had blood on them that day, but it had apparently been wiped off. He grabbed his hoodie and could smell the faint scent of his old apartment still trapped in its fibers.

"Please sign here that you have received your belongings." Clanton pushed across a clipboard with a large X where Jeremy needed to sign, and he scribbled a rusty signature. Months without writing made the pen feel foreign in his grip. If he planned to write a book about his twisted adventures, he would need to shake that feeling off.

Officer Clanton put the items back in the bag and pushed it across to Jeremy. "There's a changing room in the hallway, you can change into these clothes for your trip to Pueblo."

"Thank you," Jeremy said, getting no acknowledgment. He grabbed the bag and headed for the door, where his two escorts still stood. He paused in front of them, waiting for them to move. They both looked down at him, speechless, before moving aside to let him pass. Officer Mustache followed him and waited outside the changing room.

The changing room reminded Jeremy of his solitary room at the courthouse, a small eight-by-eight room with solid white walls and fluorescent lights that buzzed above, only this one had no window. He slid the orange jumpsuit off and watched it fall into a puddle at his feet as he stood in his county-issued boxers, feeling liberated.

Did they give these clothes back to me as some sort of sick prank? A final joke before I leave?

Jeremy pulled up his jeans and slid his feet into the shoes. The pants were a bit tight, but would be okay until he was given his new attire at the mental hospital. He stared at his gray T-shirt and black hoodie, not really wanting to put them on. He could vividly remember putting on that shirt on the morning of March 11, 2016. His mind was sharp and focused that morning as he looked around his apartment for the final time. He pulled the T-shirt over his head, an action he had forgotten after more than a year of stepping into his one-piece jumpsuit.

He picked up the hoodie and looked at it in his hands. It was a hoodie he'd worn often in the winter. Sometimes Jamie had worn it when his apartment was cold and he knew the scent of her perfume and fruity shampoo still rested somewhere within it.

"Heston! Shouldn't be taking this long!" Officer Mustache barked from the other side of the door, banging on it with a heavy fist. There were no locks and he could have let himself in had he wanted.

"Almost done!" Jeremy shouted back in a cracking voice. He started to feel nervous. Of the many instances throughout this entire process when he had felt in way over his head, his pending transfer to a mental hospital was perhaps the greatest.

He slid his arms into the hoodie and pulled it over his head, pulling the hood back from his buzzed head. He had an instant flashback to that day. The last time he'd put on this hoodie, it had been showtime. That hot sun beat down on him as he stood at the trunk of his car with King Kong—his rifle—and a duffel bag full of loaded magazines.

A surge of power rushed through him once the hoodie was snug around his body. It felt damn good to be leaving a mark on history forever. It was a lonely feeling, but a powerful one.

Jeremy picked up his jumpsuit before opening the door to Office Mustache. He extended the suit to him.

"Take it to Officer Clanton," the officer said sternly and stepped aside. Jeremy's head rose just to the guard's chest, and he saw that his name badge read *SULLIVAN*.

He took his clothes to Officer Clanton, who still refused to look him in the eyes. "Your car is here early. You'll be heading out in a couple minutes, as soon as Officer Malone is ready. Have a seat until then."

Clanton finally looked up, but past Jeremy, and nodded at the two officers standing guard. They returned the nod and left the room.

Only a minute passed before a scrawny cop entered the room. His navy blue uniform was in pristine condition, shoes shined, badge sparkling.

First day on the job?

"Mr. Heston?" Officer Malone questioned. He sounded anxious.

"Hello," Jeremy said with a smile. He decided he would be kind to everyone he met from this point forward. It could only help accelerate whatever bullshit plan they had for him in the loony bin.

"Car is ready, and so am I. Shall we head out?"

"Yes, sir, I'm ready."

Jeremy felt adrenaline start to pump, throbbing in his fingertips. His hands trembled slightly at the thought of leaving this God-awful building. He would be stepping out into the real world for an extended period of time, outside of the walls of the jail.

Two hours cruising down I-25. This guy might even let me roll the window down so I can stick my head out like a dog.

"This way, please," Malone said and turned out the door. Jeremy wondered why he hadn't been handcuffed for the drive. Did they no longer see him as a threat? Or did society actually see him as an innocent man whose own mind got in his way?

He followed Malone down a long hallway to the back of the police station. Malone signed a form for another officer standing guard at the exit and Jeremy noticed the turkey and pumpkin cutouts that decorated the hall.

It was a Thursday in late November, and after more than a year out of society, he realized it was Thanksgiving.

"This way please," Officer Malone said as he pushed open the door. A squad car waited immediately outside. He opened the back door and gestured for Jeremy to get in.

"They make you work on Thanksgiving?" Jeremy asked.

"Yeah, just one of the perks of being the new kid on the block. I don't mind though. All my family is back in Connecticut, and a newbie like me doesn't have a chance at getting a whole weekend off to go visit them."

"I see." Jeremy sat in the back seat of the cop car for the first time without handcuffs and shackles. The divider kept him separate from the front, where the radio crackled with gibberish only cops could understand.

The rookie cop took his seat behind the wheel and buckled his seatbelt. "Let's get this show on the road," he said as they pulled away from the station. Jeremy looked out his window until the large brown building disappeared from sight.

I did it. I'm out of there and not going back.

39

Chapter 39

Thursday, November 23, 2017

The drive was quiet and scenic. Once they were outside of Denver, the surroundings were mostly open fields, but the blue mountains in the distance provided a breathtaking view away from the smog of downtown. The patrol car hummed along I-25 at a steady 75. After half an hour, they were far out of Officer Malone's official jurisdiction, so he lowered the police radio's volume and turned on the FM radio to the golden voice of Freddie Mercury singing "Bohemian Rhapsody."

Malone whistled and hummed along while Jeremy stared out the window in a daze. The adrenaline faded away, leaving a twisting sense of anticipation in Jeremy as he awaited his arrival to Rocky Mountain Mental Health Institute.

"About forty-five more minutes," the young officer said as they passed through Colorado Springs. Jeremy looked out his window and saw Pike's Peak in all her glory.

The next stretch was treacherous, as the Rocky Mountains disappeared from sight thanks to the rising foothills in the area. The remainder of the drive consisted of dirt and abandoned buildings. They drove into nothingness.

Then signs of life started reappearing. Dirt gave way to greenery, billboards popped up on the side of the highway, and warehouse buildings popped up behind the truck stops.

It occurred to Jeremy that whatever way the trial had ended, he would have been on this same route. The major prison where the big shots were sent was in Cañon City, just a few minutes west of Pueblo.

Pueblo will do just fine. It's a beautiful city, he lied to himself.

The engine hummed softly as they approached their exit. The turn signal clicked on as the car turned into town, where neighborhoods and a strip mall were now in sight. Officer Malone zigzagged through the city for five minutes before passing a large shopping mall and turning down a side road. A large brick sign welcomed them to *ROCKY MOUNTAIN MENTAL HEALTH INSTITUTE: COLORADO DEPARTMENT OF HUMAN SERVICES.*

Two flagpoles stood tall behind the sign, one with the Colorado state flag and the taller one the U.S. flag, both flapping furiously in the wind.

"Here we are," Malone spoke up for the first time in almost an hour. They approached a massive brick building that stood five stories tall. A row of windows ran along each floor that stretched as long as a football field.

The car stopped at the hospital's front doors, where the electronic doors parted for a group of three nurses and a large security officer.

They were there for him. One nurse held a clipboard beneath her bosom, and the other two waited with their hands clasped in front of them.

This is my new home. The next phase is underway.

There was no press waiting, no news vans parked in the lot, no mourning family members awaiting his arrival. He was officially in the middle of nowhere and no one gave a shit about him here. The drama of the trial was over and he was now an afterthought—a footnote in America's ugly history of gun violence.

He was not the mental health champion he sought to be. Nothing had changed with regard to how the mentally ill were treated. The world carried on as normal, awaiting the chance to offer their thoughts and prayers for the next mass murder of their fellow citizens.

But Jeremy's eyes were still on the prize.

You can count on one thing for sure. I will *change the world.*

Acknowledgements

Another thank you to my editor, Teja Watson. Your attention to detail is truly appreciated, it's been a great experience working with you on this trilogy. Dane Low again with fantastic work on the cover design, I can't imagine having any one else make my covers!

Thank you to my aunts Chris, Tanya, and Maria for being early beta readers and providing strong feedback as always. Thanks to my beta and ARC team, your help is appreciated more than you'll ever know.

Thank you to my wife, Natasha, for keeping us moving forward one day at a time in this crazy journey we find ourselves in. I couldn't imagine doing this with anyone else!

And lastly, but certainly not least, thank you to Arielle and Felix. Seeing your two little faces everyday is all the motivation I need to keep chasing this dream.

See you all in the next book!

Andre Gonzalez
April 24, 2018

Thank you

Thank you for taking the time to read my work. As an independent author, receiving reviews are critical to any future success. If you enjoyed the book (or even if you didn't), I ask you to please leave it a review. You can leave reviews on Amazon or Goodreads. This will help me not only with promoting this current work, but future books as well. I appreciate you taking the time if you choose to do so!

I also look forward to connecting with my readers to discuss this book, or any book, for that matter. If you have not done so already, feel free to follow me on my social media sites and subscribe to my mailing list through my website!

www.andregonzalez.net
Facebook: www.facebook.com/AndreGonzalezAuthor
Twitter: @monitoo408
Instagram: @monitoo408
Goodreads: www.goodreads.com/AndreGonzalez

I'm always open to any discussion surrounding my work and would love to hear your thoughts!

Read a story about the Exalls (from *Followed Home*) for free at andregonzalez.net. Check out A Poisoned Mind today!

95795240R00134

Made in the USA
Columbia, SC
20 May 2018